HE WAS BECOMING A COMPLETELY DIFFERENT MAN

The doctor stared at him unsmiling, grim, "You won't be able to speak in a few days unless you spend every spare minute reading and talking just to keep those particular conditioned reflexes alive."

"What if I don't?" His lips were ash-dry.

The doctor's voice was grave. "Because, if you don't, your brain will become almost as blank as a newborn baby's. There may be"—he hesitated—"other reactions, but we don't know what. We know that you are forgetting your past at an alarming rate. . . ."

A.E. VAN VOGT

THE CHANGELING

MANOR BOOKS INC.

A MANOR BOOK

Manor Books, Inc.
432 Park Avenue South
New York, New York 10016

Copyright © 1942, 1944, by Street and Smith
Publications, Inc. for Austounding Science-Fiction
Copyright © 1950, by A. E. van Voght.
Printed in the United States of America.
ISBN: 0-532-12589-4

CHAPTER
1

"In the four years since you've been here," said Nypers, "this firm has done very well."

Craig laughed. "You will have your joke, Nypers. What do you mean, in the four years since I've been here. Why, I've been here so long, I feel like a graybeard."

Nypers nodded his thin, wise head. "I know how it is, sir. Everything else grows vague and unreal. There's a sense as if another personality has lived that past life." He turned away. "Well, I'll leave the Winthrop contract with you."

Craig finally withdrew his astounded gaze from the impassive panels of the oak door beyond which the old clerk had vanished. He shook his head wonderingly, then in self-annoyance. But he grinned as he sat down at the desk.

Nypers must be feeling his oats this morning. First time the old fellow had attempted humor.

. In the four years since you— let's see now, how long *had* he been manager of the Nesbitt Company. Office boy at sixteen; that was in 1938, junior clerk at nineteen, then the war. He'd joined up in April, 1942, been wounded, hospitalized and sent home early in '44. Back to the Nesbitt Company to become successively senior clerk in 1949, office manager in '53, and general manager in '60. Since then, well, the days in an office were pretty much alike. Time blew by like a steady north wind.

Here it was, 1972. Hm-m-m, thirty-four years with the firm, not counting the war; twelve as general manager. That made him exactly fifty this year.

Fifty?

With a cry, Craig leaped to his feet, and raced into the washroom adjoining his private office. There was a full-length mirror in the door of the glittering shower booth. He paused in front of it, breathlessly. The image that met his gaze was satisfyingly familiar. It was that of a tall, powerfully built young man about six feet tall and thirty-three or four years of age.

Craig recovered his calmness. One of those perpetual juvenile types, he told himself in amusement. Didn't look a day over forty. Odd though, that it had never occurred to him that he was fifty. He allowed himself a glow of pleasure at the realization that he was holding up so well. Anrella, too, for that matter. If he didn't look forty, she didn't look thirty.

His mind faltered. He went back into the office and sat down heavily in his chair. *In the four years since you've been with us—* The words made a pattern in his mind. The action he took finally was semi-automatic. He pressed a button on his desk.

The door opened and a scrawny, white-faced woman of thirty-five or so came in.

"You called, Mr. Craig?"

Craig hesitated. He was beginning to feel foolish, and not a little amazed at his upset. "Miss Pearson," he said, "how long have you been with the Nesbitt Company?"

The woman looked at him sharply; and Craig remembered too late that in these days of aggressive feminine emancipation, an employer didn't ask a female employee questions that might be construed as not being related to business.

After a moment, Miss Pearson's eyes lost their hard hostile gleam; and Craig breathed easier. "Nine years!" she said curtly.

"Who," Craig forced himself to say, "hired you?"

Miss Pearson shrugged, but the gesture must have been in connection with something in her own mind. Her voice was normal as she said, "Why, the then manager, Mr. Letstone."

"Oh!" said Craig.

He almost pointed out that he had been general manager for the past twelve years. He didn't, mainly because the thought behind the words simply skittered off into vagueness. His mind poised blank, but relatively unconfused. The idea that came finally was logical and unblurred. He voiced it in a calm tone:

"Bring me the Personnel Accounts book for 1968, please."

"Yes, Mr. Craig."

She brought the book and laid it on his desk. When she had gone out, Craig opened the volume at SALARIES for the month of October. And there it was: "Lesley Craig, general manager, $1250."

September had the same entry. Impatient, he thumbed back to January. It read:

"Angus Letstone, general manager, $700."

There was no explanation for the lower pay. February, March, April were all Angus Letstone. All at $700 a month.

In May, the name of Lesley Craig appeared for the first time at $1250.

Four years! In the four years since you—

The Winthrop contract lay unread on the great oak desk. Craig stood up, and went over and stared out of the vitreous glass windows that made a curving design at the corner of the room. A broad avenue spread below him, a tree-lined boulevard that glittered with marble buildings. Money had flowed into this street—and into this room. He thought of how often he had believed himself one of those fortunate men at the lower end of the big income class, a man who had attained the top position in his company after years of toil.

Ruefully, Craig shook his head. The years of toil hadn't occurred. The question therefore was: how had he got this excellent job with its pleasant salary, its exclusive clientele, its smoothly operating organization? Life had been as lovely and sweet as a drink of clear, cold water, an untroubled idyll, a simple design of happy living.

And now this!

How did a man find out what he had done during the first forty-six years of his life? Especially, how did he find it out when he didn't look forty-six—let alone fifty— by more than a dozen years? There were a few simple facts that he could verify before taking any action. With abrupt decision he returned to his desk, picked up his dictaphone, and began:

"Records Department, War Office, Washington, D.C. Dear Sir: Please send as soon as possible my record for World War II. I was in the—"

He explained in detail, gathering confidence as he went along. His memory was so very clear on the main facts. The actual army life, the battles, were vague and far away. But that was understandable. There was that trip Anrella and he had taken to Canada last year. It was a dim dream now, with only here and there flashes of mental pictures to verify that it had ever happened.

All life was a process of forgetting the past.

His second letter he addressed to Birth Record Statistics, Chicago, Illinois. "I was born," he dictated, "on June 1, 1922, in the town of Daren, Illinois. Please send my birth certificate as soon as possible."

He rang for Miss Pearson, and gave her the dictaphone record when she came in. "Verify those addresses," he instructed briskly. "I believe there's some small charge involved. Find out what, enclose money orders and send both letters air mail."

He felt pleased with himself when she had gone out. No use getting excited about this business. After all, here he was, solid in his job, his mind as steady as a rock. There was no reason to let himself become upset, and even less cause for allowing others to discover his predicament. In due course the answers to his two letters would arrive. Time enough then to pursue the matter further.

He picked up the Winthrop contract and began to read it.

Twenty minutes later, it struck him with a shock that he had spent most of the time striving to remember just what he had been doing during May, 1968. That was the month the first rocket had reached the moon. Mentally, Craig pictured the newspaper headlines as he had seen them. And there was no doubt. He *had* seen them. They loomed in his mind, big and black. He could regard May, his first month with the Nesbitt Company— according to the salary records—as part of the continuity of his present existence.

What about April? In April there had been the internal squabble that had nearly split wide open the powerful union of women's clubs. And the headlines had been—what? Craig strained to remember, but nothing came. He thought: what about May 1st? If April's end and May's beginning had been the dividing line, then May 1st should perhaps have some special quality of aliveness that would mark it as sharply as a lover's first kiss. He had, he remembered vaguely, been sick about that time.

His mind wouldn't pin down that first day of the month of May. Presumably he had had breakfast. Presumably he had gone to the office after receiving one of Anrella's lingering good-by kisses. His mind poised in mid-flight like an animal that has been shot on the run. Anrella! he thought. She must have been there on April 30th and 29th and in March, February, January, and back and back.

There was not in his whole memory the suggestion, nor had there been in her actions during the vital month of May, that they hadn't been married for years.

Therefore—*Anrella knew!*

It was a realization that had its emotional limitations. The curious dartings of his mind at the first sharp awareness of the idea were caught in the net of a quieter logic, and grew calm. So Anrella knew. Well, so she ought. He had obviously been around for many years. Any change that had occurred had taken place in his mind, not in hers.

Craig glanced at the wall clock: a quarter to twelve. He'd just have time to drive home for lunch. He usually had lunch in town, but the information he wanted couldn't wait.

A number of good-looking women were standing in the hallway as he headed for the elevator. The impression thaththey stared at him sharply as he passed was so strong that Craig was torn out of his own tempestuous thoughts. He turned and glanced back.

One of the women was saying something into a little, shining device on her wrist. Craig thought, interested, "A magic jewel radio."

He was in the elevator then, and he forgot the incident during the space of the downward trip. There were women in the lobby as he emerged from the elevator, and still others in the entranceway. At the curb stood half a dozen imposing black cars with a woman driver behind each steering wheel. In a few minutes the street would be swarming with the noon rush crowds. But now, except for the women, it was almost deserted.

"Mr. Craig?"

Craig turned. It was one of the young women who had been standing just outside the doorway, a brisk-looking woman with a strangely stern face.

Craig stared at her. "Uh!" he said.

"You are Mr. Lesley Craig?"

Craig emerged further out of his half-reverie. "Why, yes, I . . . what—"

"O.K., girls," said the young woman.

Amazingly, guns appeared. They glittered metallically in the sun. Before Craig could more than blink at them hands caught his arms and propelled him toward one of the limousines. He could have resisted. But he didn't. He had no sense of danger. In his brain was simply an enormous, paralyzing astonishment. He was inside the car, and the machine was moving, before his mind resumed its functioning.

"Say, look here!" he began.

"Please do not ask any questions, Mr. Craig." It was the young woman who had already spoken to him; she sat now at his right. "You are not going to be hurt—unless you misbehave."

As if to illustrate the threat, the two women who sat on small pull-down center seats facing him with drawn guns wiggled their shiny weapons meaningfully.

After a minute, it was still not a dream.

Craig said, "Where are you taking me?"

"Ask no questions. Please!"

That brought impatience, a sense of being treated like a child. Grim, furious, Craig leaned back and with hostile eyes studied his captors. They were typical, short-skirted "new" women. The two gun-women looked well over forty, yet they were slenderly, lithely built. Their eyes had the very bright look of women who had taken the Equalizer—Makes you the Equal of a Man—drug treatment. The young leader, and the girl on Craig's left, had the same bright-eyed appearance.

They all looked capable.

Before Craig could think further, the machine twisted around a corner and up a long, slanting incline of pavement. Craig had time to recognize that this was the garage entrance to the skyscraper McCandless Hotel, and then they were inside the garage and sweeping toward a distant door.

The car stopped. Without a word, Craig obeyed the pistols that motioned him out. He was led along a deserted corridor to a freight elevator. The elevator halted at the third floor. Surrounded by his all-women guard, Craig was herded slantwise across the gleaming corridor and through a door.

The room was large and lovely, and magnificently furnished. At the far end, on a green lounge, his back to an enormous window, sat a fine-looking, gray-haired man.

To the man's right, at a desk, sat a young woman. Craig scarcely glanced at the latter. Wide-eyed, he watched as the youthful leader of his guards approached the gray-haired man and said:

"As you requested, President Dayles, we have brought you Mr. Lesley Craig."

It was the name, so blandly spoken, that confirmed the identification. Incredulous, he had already recognized the much-photographed face. There was no further room for doubt. Here was Jefferson Dayles, President of the United States.

Anger gone, Craig stared at the great man. He was aware of the women who had escorted him leaving the room. Their departure pointed up the strangeness of this forced interview.

The man, he saw, was studying him narrowly. Craig noticed that, except for the gray eyes that glowed like ash-colored pearls, President Dayles looked his publicized age of fifty-nine. Newspaper photographs had suggested a youthful, unlined face. But it was clear, gazing at him from this short distance, that the strain of this second campaign was taking its toll of the man's life force.

Nevertheless, the president's countenance was unmistakably strong, commanding and handsome, with a serenity of assurance. His voice, when he spoke, had all the glowing, resonant power that had contributed so much to his great success. He said with the faintest of sardonic smiles, "What do you think of my amazons?"

His laughter rolled Homerically through the room. He obviously expected no answer, for his amusement ended abruptly and he went on without pause, "A very curious manifestation, these women. And, I think, a typically American manifestation at that. Once taken, the drug cannot be counteracted; and I regard it as an evidence of the basic will-to-adventure of American girls that some thousands took the treatment. Unfortunately, it brought them to a dead end, left them futureless. Unequalized women dislike them, and men think they're 'queer', to use a colloquialism. Their existence did serve the purpose of galvanizing the women's clubs into undertaking a presidential campaign. But as individuals, the amazons discovered that no employer would hire them, and no man would marry them.

"In desperation, their leaders approached me; and just before the situation reached the tragic stage, I arranged a skillful preliminary publicity, and hired them *en masse* for what is generally believed to be perfectly legitimate purposes. Actually, these women know their benefactor, and regard themselves as peculiarly my personal agents."

Jefferson Dayles paused, then went on blandly, "I hope, Mr. Craig, that this will explain to some extent the odd method by which you were brought before me. Miss Kay Whitewood"—he motioned to the young woman at the desk—"is their intellectual leader."

Craig did not let his gaze follow the gesturing hand. He stood like a stone, and was almost as blank mentally. He had listened to the brief history of the group of amazons with a fascinated sense of unreality. For the story explained nothing. It wasn't the means, or the details of how he had been brought here that counted. It was why?

He saw that the fine eyes were smiling at him in amusement. Jefferson Dayles said quietly, "There is a possibility that you will wish to report what has happened to authorities or newspapers. Kay, give Mr. Craig the news item we have prepared to meet such an eventuality."

The young woman rose from the chair at the desk, and came around it toward Craig. Standing up, she looked older. She had blue eyes, and a very hard, pretty face. She handed Craig a sheet with typewritten lines on it. He read:

Big Town—July 9, 1972—An irritating incident disturbed President Jefferson Dayle's motor drive from Middle City. What seemed like an attempt to ram the President's car on the part of a young man in an electric automobile was frustrated by the prompt action of his guards. The young man was taken into custody, and later brought to the presidential hotel suite for questioning. His explanations were considered satisfactory. Accordingly, at President Dayles request, no charges were made, and he was released.

After a moment, Craig allowed himself a curt laugh. This doctored news item was, of course, final. He could no more engage in a newspaper duel with Jefferson Dayles than he could, well, ride up Main Street firing a six-shooter. Mentally, he pictured the shouting headlines:

OBSCURE BUSINESS MAN ACCUSES JEFFERSON DAYLES

Smear Campaign Against the President

Craig laughed again, more sardonically this time. There seemed little doubt. Whatever Jefferson Dayles' reason for having him kidnapped—his mind poised there. Whatever his reason! What *could* be his reason? Bewildered, he shook his head. He could contain himself no longer. His gaze fixed on the gray, half-amused eyes of the executive. "All this," he marvelled, "so much effort expended, such a dishonorable story deliberately prepared—for what?"

It seemed to him then, as he stared at the other, that the interview was about to get down to business.

The older man cleared his throat, and said, "Mr. Craig, can you name the major inventions perfected since the end of World War II?"

He stopped. Craig waited for him to go on. But the silence lengthened, and the president continued to look at him patiently. Craig was startled. It apparently was a genuine question, not just rhetoric. He shrugged, and said, "Well, there hasn't been much. Of course, I'm not up on these things, but I would say the rocket to the moon, and a few developments of the radio tube and—" He broke off, blankly, "But see here, what is all this? What—"

The firm voice caught at one of his sentences. "There hasn't been much, you say. That statement, Mr. Craig, is the most tragic commentary imaginable on the state of our world. There-hasn't-been-much. You mention rockets. Man, we don't dare tell the world that the rocket, except for minor details, was perfected during the war, and that it's taken us thirty years to solve those minor details."

He had leaned forward, in the intensity of his argument. Now, he sank back with a sigh. "Mr. Craig, some people say that the cause of this incredible stagnation of the human mind is the direct result of the kind of world that came out of World War II. That, I think, is partly to blame. A bad moral atmosphere tires the mind in a curious, sustained fashion; it is hard to describe. It is as if the brain wears itself out fighting its intellectual environment."

He paused, and sat frowning, as if he was searching for a more definitive description. Craig had time to think in amazement: Why was *he* being given this intimate, detailed argument?

The executive looked up. He seemed to be unaware that he had paused. He went on, "But that is only part of the reason. You mentioned radio tubes." He repeated in an oddly helpless voice, "Radio tubes!" He smiled wearily. "Mr Craig, one of my degrees is a B.Sc., and that has made me aware of the tremendous problem confronting modern technology, the problem of the impossibility of one man learning all there is to know about one science.

"But to get back to radio tubes—it is not generally known that for several years a number of famous laboratories have been picking up weak radio signals which are believed to originate on Mars. Six months ago, I determined to find out why no progress was being made towards amplifying these signals. I invited three of the greatest men in their special radio fields to explain to me what was wrong.

"One of these men designs tubes, another circuits, the third man tries to make the finished article out of the separate jobs of the other two. The trouble is this: tubes are a lifetime study. The tube designer cannot but be hazy on circuits because that, too, is a lifetime study. The circuit man has to take what tubes he can get because, having only a theoretical knowledge of tubes, he cannot specify or even imagine what a tube should do in order to fulfill the purpose he has in mind. Among them those three men have the knowledge to construct new and startingly powerful radios. But over and over and over again they fail. They cannot conjoin their knowledges. They—"

He must have become aware of the expression on Craig's face. He stopped, and with a faint smile, said, "Are you following me, Mr. Craig?"

Craig bowed before the ironical twist in the other's smile. The long monologue had given him time to gather his thoughts. He said, "The picture I'm visualizing is this: A small business man has been forcibly picked up on the street and brought before the president of the United States. The president immediately launches into a lecture on radio tubes. Sir, it doesn't make sense. What do you want from me?"

The answer came slowly, "For one thing, I wanted to have a look at you. For another—"

21

Jefferson Dayles paused; then, "What is your blood type, Mr. Craig?"

"Why, I—" Craig caught himself, and stared at the man. "My what?"

"I want a sample of your blood," said the president. He turned to the girl, "Kay," he said, "obtain the sample, will you? I'm sure Mr. Craig will not resist."

Craig didn't. He allowed his hand to be taken. The needle jabbed his thumb, bringing a faint stab of pain. He watched curiously as the red blood flowed up the narrow tube of the needle.

"That's all," said the president. "Good-by, Mr. Craig. It was pleasant meeting you. Kay, will you please call Mabel and have her return Mr. Craig to his office."

Mabel was apparently the name of the leader of his escort, for it was she who came into the room, followed by the gunwomen. In a minute, Craig was out in the hall, and in the elevator.

After Craig had gone, the great man sat with a fixed smile on his face. He looked once over at the woman, but she was staring down at her desk. Slowly, Jefferson Dayles turned, and gazed at a screen that stood in the corner near the window behind him. He said quietly:

"All right, Mr. Nypers, you can come out."

Nypers must have been waiting for the signal. He appeared before the words were completed, and walked briskly over to the chair the president indicated. Jefferson Dayles waited until the old man's fingers lay idly on the ornamental metallic knobs of the chair arms; then softly:

"Mr. Nypers, you swear that what you have told us is the truth?"

"Every word." The old man spoke energetically. "Lesley Craig, though he has no knowledge of the fact, is due once more to enter his toti-potent stage. I came to you because you're his blood type AB, or group IV by Jansky nomenclature. That is your blood type, is it not?"

Jefferson Dayles did not reply. His impulse was to close his eyes against brightness. But the brightness was in his brain, not outside; and he had the shaky conviction that it could burn out his mind if he was not careful. At last he managed to turn to Kay. Relieved, he saw that she was looking up from the lie detector register on her desk. The detector was connected to the ornamental knobs on the arm of the chair in which Nypers sat. As he looked at her, Kay nodded ever so slightly.

Jefferson Dayles froze. The brightness was like a white fire; and he had to fight, to sit there rigid, straining with his brain against the unnamable joy that was tearing at his reason. The desire came to rush over to Kay's desk and glare down at the lie detector register and compel Nypers to repeat his words. But that, too, he fought off. He grew aware that Nypers was speaking again.

"Any further questions before I leave?"

"Yes." It was Kay. "What I'd like to know is, why are you doing this?"

The old man hesitated, then sighed. "I am not prepared to answer that. The reasons for a betrayal do not always sound nice when brought out into the open."

Kay's flinty blue eyes flashed. "We are unshockable, I assure you."

Nypers shrugged. "Proceed to your next question, please."

"You won't answer?"

"You have my reply."

There was silence. Jefferson Dayles saw that Kay was trying to catch his eye. He ignored the attempt. It was strange, but he felt no interest. The main fact was verified. The lie detector had proved all that was necessary. He wondered if this was so big a thing for him personally that he had already lost all objectivity in connection with it. He listened quietly as Kay said venomously:

"We could force an answer, Mr. Nypers."

The old man rose slowly to his feet. He had, Jefferson Dayles saw, an odd expression on his face. "Don't you think," he said, "that President Dayles' political situation is precarious enough without any dramatic developments?"

"What do you mean?"

It was a bad question for Kay to have asked,

24

Jefferson Dayles realized. Nypers smiled, and said softly, "There are people who maintain that the United States twenty-five years ago suffered a moral disaster as a result of World War II. A president with dictatorial ambitions opposed by a woman candidate may or may not be a proof of that." His smile deepened into a sneer. "The real proof will be the next election. How many ballot boxes have you decided to stuff in order to insure President Dayle's re-election?

"Wait!" His voice rose in pitch. "I expect you to refrain from torturing or threatening me, and to look after me according to our agreement. I expect it because I have prepared a very interesting account of this whole matter, which will come to light if anything should happen to me." He bowed, finished in a quieter voice, "I am sorry to have to be so blunt, but it is well to clarify the situation. And now, if you have no further objections, I shall depart."

This time Jefferson Dayles allowed Kay to catch his eye. He nodded, with a twisted smile. "Let him go, Kay."

At the door, Kay said to Nypers, "This toti-potent phase of Craig—what is he like when he is in it?"

"His condition varies," was the cool reply. "But"— Nypers showed gleaming white teeth—"I would not be here if he were dangerous."

"Which," said Kay savagely after the door

had closed behind Nypers, "means exactly nothing. He's holding back vital information. I'll wager the group behind him know he came here. I'll even go so far as to say that they sent him. What's their game?"

Her eyes narrowed with calculation. Several times she seemed on the verge of speaking, but each time cut her words off by an odd trick of compressing her lips.

Jefferson Dayles watched the interplay of emotions on the intensely alive face, briefly absorbed by this curious woman who felt everything so violently. Finally, he shook his head; his voice was strong as he said:

"Kay, it doesn't matter. Don't you see that? Their game, as you call it, means nothing. No one, no individual, no group, can stand up against the commander-in-chief of the United States Army, Navy and Air Force." He drew a deep, slow breath. "Don't you realize, Kay, that the world is ours?"

CHAPTER
2

Craig sat in a restaurant, eating. His hands with the fork and knife in them, or a piece of bread, or a cup, moved up and down, like synchronized robot attachments of his body. The food touched his lips, and there was an occasional thrill of taste pleasure.

The two events of the morning seesawed in Craig's mind, each in turn struggling to his attention, gaining it, then yielding to the other. Gradually, the episode of Jefferson Dayles began to lose fascination. Because it meant nothing. It was like an accident happening to a man crossing a street, having no connection with the normal continuity of his life, and quickly forgotten once the shock and the pain were ended.

The rest, the problem of what had happened four years before, was different. It was still a part of his mind and his body. It was *of* him, not to be dismissed by the casual assumption that somebody must be crazy. Craig glanced at his wrist watch. It showed ten minutes to one. He pushed away his dessert and stood up. He had been heading home with the intention of obtaining explanations when the incident of Jefferson Dayles had interrupted. There was still time to go and question Anrella. But first, back to the office.

He went as far as the information desk. "Tell Mr. Nypers, when he comes in, that I'll be later than usual."

The girl answered brightly, "Mr Nypers said he wouldn't be back before three, Mr. Craig."

"Very well, then, tell Mr. Carson."

His mind persisted in remaining blank during the trip. It was as he turned his electric automobile through the massive iron gates, and saw the mansion, that a new realization struck him. This house had been here also four years ago.

It was an amazingly expensive place, with an outdoor swimming pool and landscaped grounds that he had got according to his memory, at the bargain price of ninety thousand dollars. It had not occurred to him before to wonder how he had saved ninety thousand dollars to pay for the house. The sum had somehow seemed within his means.

The residence grew from the ground. The architect must have been an earnest disciple of Frank Lloyd Wright, for the skyline blended with the trees and land. There were sturdy chimneys, outjutting wings that merged coherently with the central structure and a generous use of casement windows.

Anrella had always looked after the accounts from their joint bank control. The arrangement left him free to devote his spare time to his lust for reading, his occasional golf, his fishing and hunting trips, his private airfield with its electric plane. And, of course, it left him free for his job. But it failed to provide him with any real idea of where he stood financially.

Again, and stronger now, he realized how odd it was that he had never worried, or wondered, about the arrangement. He parked the car and walked into the house, thinking, "I'm a perfectly normal well-to-do business man who's run up against something that doesn't quite fit. I'm sane. I have nothing to win or lose physically by any inquiry. My life is ahead of me, and not behind me."

It wouldn't, he told himself forcibly, matter whether he ever learned anything, or not. The past didn't count. He could live the rest of his life with scarcely more than a twinge of curiosity—Where the devil was Nickson? Hat in hand, he stood in the great hallway waiting for the butler to acknowledge by his presence the sound of the door opening.

But no one came. Silence lay over the great house. He pressed buttons, but there was no answer. Craig tossed his hat onto a hall seat, peered into the deserted living room, and then headed for the kitchen.

"Sybil," he began irritably, "I want—"

He stopped. The reverberations of his voice echoed back at him from an empty kitchen. Nor was there any sign in the storeroom of the cook and the two pretty kitchen maids. A few minutes later Craig was climbing the main staircase when a sound of murmuring voices touched his ears.

The sound came from the upstairs drawing room. His hand was on the knob, when a spasmodic silence inside was broken by the clear voice of Anrella saying, "Really, the argument is quite useless. The time for the change has come, and it's too late now to alter our plans. Objections should have been made at the last meeting because...tell them what you did this morning, Mr. Nypers."

Nypers! The shock almost burned Craig as it struck along his nerves. The old man's dry voice came then, confirmingly, "I have done everything I was commissioned to do at our last meeting. Unsettling Mr. Craig was simple enough, but the interview with President Dayles involved, as we suspected, a careful phrasing of answers to counteract a lie detector. I think I put it over, although I have no doubt they are suspicious of us all. I'm sorry I didn't know there would be objections. But I sincerely think delay would not have been wise. The time to inform the president was while he was here on the spot, able to have Mr. Craig brought before him."

There was silence; then somebody said, "If it's done, it's done."

There followed a jumble of voices, of discussion, from which only occasional words emerged clearly: "...His great stage...the final chance...necessary to subject him to breaking pressures...think his way out of that...no limit—" Though the words made no joint sense, Craig recognized some of the voices: Peter Yerd, one of the millionaire customers of the Nesbitt Company, Nesbitt himself, a multimillionaire named Shore, Sybil the cook and—

Afterwards, Craig cursed himself for leaving at that point. But he couldn't help it. Fear came like a blinding stab of darkness, the fear that he would be discovered here, now, before he could think about what he had heard. He slipped down the stairs like a ghost, snatched his hat— As he emerged into the open, he saw for the first time the half dozen cars parked at the far side of the house. He'd been too intent on himself to notice them when he came in.

The electric automobile started with a faint hum—thank Heaven the upstairs drawing

room was on the other side of the mansion—
and a few minutes later he was guiding the
machine through the iron gates, and along the
old farmer's road to the city highway. He had
a very strong conviction that it was going to
be an afternoon of mental turmoil.

Actually, as it turned out, he was too busy to
think much. And during his lax moments his
mind kept going blank. For the first time in
years, he would have welcomed an afternoon
nap.

That night, the attendant of the building's
parking lot said to him, "A mechanic, a man
named Gregory, came to work on your car this
afternoon, Mr. Craig. I hope it was all right."

"Oh, yes, yes," Craig replied absently. He
walked on, and climbed into his machine. As
he drove off, his mind drew free of the welter of
thoughts that were in it, and focussed on the
attendant's words. After a moment, there was
still nothing to think about them. If Jim
Gregory had decided the car needed attention,
then it did.

Click! said the car fifteen minutes later. The
low, sustained humming of the engine
changed its tune; the machine slowed and
coasted to a halt. Craig frowned at the
instrument board. Then he fingered the main
switch. It was in, registering contact. He
pressed the accelerator again. No response.
Craig shook his head. This was the first time
this had ever happened. After Gregory had

gone over the engine too.

He thought about that a little harder; and slowly a chill crept over him. He sat then, remembering that Gregory was one of them. This car stalling here was no accident.

Uneasily, Craig examined his environment. He had left the highway ten minutes before, and was now in the tree-sheltered valley beyond One-mile Hill. The outskirts of the city were about eight miles behind him, the city itself no longer visible. He was roughly five miles from home, and about a mile from the nearest farmhouse.

It must have been done with a purpose. Perhaps he was expected to do something. He climbed down into the road, and then stood indecisive. He knew nothing about electric motors. Or any other kind of motor. He frowned, and reluctantly lifted the hood. He stood then, nonplussed, studying the long, narrow, streamlined shape that was under it.

There were no visible wires, and no electric motor, simply that gray metal tube about a foot and a half in diameter. Craig reached down gingerly and touched the metal. Instantly, he jerked his hand back—but forced it down again, touched the metal, even more swiftly this time. And there was no doubt. The metal was cold *cold*. Unnaturally, icily cold! Freezingly, deathly cold.

Craig put down the hood, and stood there on that quiet road, stood very still and very tense.

But it was only after a long blankness that he realized the truth. This was it. This was what they had wanted him to find out. Nypers had given him the first hint that something was wrong. This was supposed to be the second.

Actually, of course, he had already overheard, and guessed, much. But they didn't know that.

For years he had believed his car had an electric motor powering it; and now they wanted him to know that the motor wasn't electric at all. That instead it was—

What?

Gregory picked him up at the farm house about fifteen minutes after Craig phoned. He was a big, powerfully built young man with a placid face. He said easily, "I could have sworn there was something wrong with the car when you left this morning, Mr. Craig. Ran into town special to have a look at it, but couldn't find nothing. Guess I'll have to unwind the armature."

Craig muttered something about leaving all that to you, Jim. He was silent on the way home. Silent and shocked and uncertain. It was one thing to think, as he had earlier that Jim was a member of the gang. It was another to watch him drive up in the replica of the stalled car, and listen to his cheerful lying. To see him face to face, and *listen* to his lying.

The bitterness faded slowly before a thought that he had deliberately buried deep, but which now inexorably rose to the surface. The engine didn't fit in this picture. It had no more meaning than the action of Jefferson Dayles in having him kidnaped.

Craig found himself listening tautly to the humming sound of the motor. He had always taken for granted that the vague throb was that of an electric engine. It was similar. But it seemed to him suddenly that it was throatier. Could it be compressed air? But then why had they lied to him? He who knew nothing about either motive force would have accepted an air-pressure engine explanation with the same credulity that he had accepted the statement that the power was electric.

It would be different if the engine was something marvelous. But it wasn't. It drove a plane at a cruising speed of ninety-five miles an hour and a car at a top speed of eighty. That was so, at least, according to the speedometer. He had never tested the capacity.

Inwardly, Craig groaned. The wretched thing about it all was, how was he expected to react? For some reason or other, they had not expected him to be so troubled that he would drive home for lunch. As a result, he knew more than they realized. It would be difficult under such circumstances to know what to say, even to Anrella.

Should he be bold? Cautious? Demanding? Secretive?

It was a problem.

Her kiss was sweet and prolonged. Her mouth was warm, her manner ardent. Her fingers brushed his cheeks in a caressing gesture, as she finally half-released him, half-withdrew from his responsive embrace. It was briefly hard to remember that he had heard her say in a resonant, resolute voice—what she had said to the people gathered in the drawing room that noon.

Anrella stared at him now, and said, "You look tired, darling. Come into the living room and lie down. I'm sorry you had the trouble with the car. I shall have to speak sharply to Gregory."

He watched her from the sofa with appraising eyes. And it shocked him to realize that she looked quite capable of speaking sharply to Gregory. Or to anybody else for that matter. She had eyes of deep blue, and a figure that was tall and, well, svelte. She was easy on the eyes, this wife of his; and it wasn't that she looked cruel. She merely looked mature. Tremendously mature for one physically so young.

It was the kind of maturity you might expect from a matron of fifty. Young women were usually very careful of the way they exercised authority. Maids, gardeners, clerks, male or female, had a habit of quitting if a thirty-year-old woman was too bossy.

Somehow, Anrella carried it off. None of her

help had ever quit for any reason. That is, quit for good. They simply took long holidays and, suddenly, there they were again, looking tanned and healthy, as if they had been to Palm Beach, or Miami, or somewhere. Craig paused on the idle thought, startled. *Could* they have been to Palm Beach?

He shook himself impatiently, but his almost closed eyes widened a little. He watched Anrella where she sat in a nearby chair glancing through the evening paper he had brought.

Palm Beach was improbable, of course. But where did they go? It was an angle that might be worth investigating. And there were other things. For instance, what wages did Anrella pay? In an outfit that included millionaires like Yerd but also Sybil the cook, and Gregory, it was just as well to gather a few facts before mentioning anything. He didn't know enough. He—didn't—know!

He watched Anrella from slitted eyes. How sleek she was, how beautifully dressed. She was like that mentally, too; always, hers had been a richly garbed mind, swift in response, and in a curious, hard yet intensely human and humane logic.

Whatever else happened, he must draw her safely clear.

If only he had the courage to question her. But, no!—decisively though imperceptibly, Craig shook his head. Not now. Wait! There would be time enough after he had a more solid base of information. Somehow, she had got entangled into a powerful organization, and the will to help her would never be enough. Not the will of a man who hadn't the faintest real idea what his own past history was.

He must never forget that the tremendous gap in his mind had to come first. Astonishing as his other discoveries had been, they were yet not as important as the false past that had been impressed on his brain. He had to live with his mind. So long as it remained partially blank, his life would be an empty shell.

They knew, of course, that he knew something. Let them. Let them wonder how he was taking it, what he was doing and thinking. If he showed no sign, they would become puzzled, and wonder if perhaps he had not missed their cues. Further action on their part would then be inevitable. By playing dumb, but not too dumb, he might reach the point where he knew enough to act. The point, for instance, where he knew exactly how Jefferson Dayles fitted into the picture.

Somehow, all this was connected.

It wasn't fear; Jefferson Dayles knew that. But he had to have, for the sake of his nerves and his conscience, *had* to have Craig safe.

This council of war had no other purpose. But for a while Jefferson Dayles temporized.

He emphasized to the women, as he had in a previous meeting, that his re-election chances were dimming by the hour. As he stared out over the small pond of hard, bright, alarmed faces, he felt anew the close-knittedness of his relationship with these leaders of America's equalized women.

They were his, body and soul, almost like personal possessions, or extensions of his own physique—his private army in a world where, since Hitler, there had been a strong prejudice against anyone in politics who gathered such a force around him. But no one suspected how completely they were his creatures. Not even his political opponents who, after careful prodding, announced acidly through the medium of Mrs. Janet Wake herself, that they would certainly not tolerate equalized women in the government service "if I am elected president."

His speech to them now was a preliminary, a building up to his main theme: Craig. He said:

"We are living in a curious age, an age where people jump this way, that way, without thought. Right now they are in the throes of an ecstatic will to give women equality by electing Janet Wake as the first woman president. It is an unreasoned determination because it is basically at odds with reality. If women as a body were prepared to take the equalizer drug, and if men could get over their instinctive dislike of women who have taken it, the problem might be resolved.

"But as you equalized women know from you personal experience, women are your worst enemies, and men won't have anything to do with you. If normal women start running this country after a successful election, there will be chaos and riots, immense revulsions of feeling, rancor unprecedented—"

He believed every word of that. Preliminary though all this was, it was the essence of his convictions that was pressing out of his voice. Subtly, he shifted his line of argument, conscious that even these ostracized women had to be handled right, to make them forget they were women who, under normal conditions, would be vociferous supporters of a woman president.

"The mass of people, with their love of simple slogans, are almost completely unaware that the only reason why democracy is a good system is because it provides opportunities to eliminate bad and tyrannical governments. Democracy enables the people to knock out of office the most flagrant of two or more power grasping groups, thus exercising a wholesome restraint over their lusts.

"Actually, what democracy does is create a temporary benevolent dictatorship. The administration, with its special powers, is virtually a law unto itself during its term of office. The danger, the immense and deadly danger, where the dictatorship is not legally temporary, has been that sooner or later the good dictator has died, to be succeeded by a bloody, stupid tyrant with schemes for war and personal aggrandizement. I shall be a benevolent immortal dictator—"

Dayles believed that, too, the benevolent part. For years and years he had been, in spite of all his friends and colleagues, alone in the world. He had made the mistake in 1944 of taking Alice and the boys to London; and one bomb had blotted them from his life. It was all vauge now. It was hard in these days to think with any sense of reality of the young woman who had been his wife. For nearly thirty years he had watched the changing shape of a badly mauled world, had watched science stagger blindly to a halt, shackled by the mortality of the poor, miserable human beings who learned just so much, then sank into their graves, taking their knowledge with them.

The blood of Lesley Craig, carefully allotted, would end all that. He knew what must be done, what could be done. Sometimes he admitted wryly that power was sweet in itself, and life precious. But, most often, he felt selfless.

He said, "In view of the necessity for ballot box stuffing on such a large scale, I have come to the conclusion that only the certainty of success would make it all justifiable. We must have Craig now, not as we originally planned, after the election. It's risky; it will be personally dangerous for all of us. Discovery would ruin my re-election chances, and end our hopes. Nevertheless, there is no evading the issues.

"A dictator must convince the citizens of the country he rules that he is wonderful, unique, supra-normal. What greater wonder than if, at the end of my second term, the Hand of God seems to reach down and slough thirty years from my age? It will seem a blessing from heaven itself. The religious fervor that will sweep the land will jump the oceans and win us the whole world. I shall, if we plan well, automatically be accepted as the permanent president of the United States.

"But we must have the man who can make that possible. Even though it is months yet to the election, we must have Craig. I want arrangements made to insure his capture within a month."

Afterward, just before bedtime, he spoke briefly, privately to Kay. "Did you tell them what I asked you to?" he said.

She nodded a little stiffly. "I don't think they have much hope. They can see all right that Craig can, during one thirty-year period, rejuvenate about three hundred people. But they don't quite believe that any amount of scientific manipulation can benefit people who are not of his blood type."

Jefferson Dayles hesitated; then, "Suppose

42

it couldn't be done, what would you think personally?"

"There's nothing to think about," was the harsh reply. "I'm not his or your blood type, whether they call it AB, Moss 1 or Jansky IV, and that's all there is to it. Besides—"

"Yes?" He spoke softly.

"I'm only thirty-four. When I get older, I may start cursing fate. I don't think about it very often."

There was silence, then: "Good night, Kay."

"Good night."

CHAPTER
3

The days ran their swift course, and life went on. Every morning except Sunday, Craig climbed into his—not electric—runabout, and drove to work. Every evening except Sunday—and Saturday, when he left at one—he drove back again to the great house inside the iron fence.

It required a real effort of will not to change his hours or his route. Particularly his route. The more he thought about the way his car had stalled on that lonely farmer's road in dense bush country a mile from the nearest farm, the more desirable the highway through Alcina seemed. But he didn't dare change to it. It would be noticed. They'd know then that he had seen the engine.

Craig wanted tensely for their reaction to his non-reaction. But nothing happened.

On the seventh morning, the letter arrived containing his birth certificate. Craig read it with satisfaction and, he admitted it frankly to himself, relief.

There it was in black and white: "Lesley Somers Craig. Born June 1, 1922, town of Daren, county of Goose Lake. Father: John Laidlaw Craig. Mother: Grace Rosemary Somers—"

He had been born. His memory had not played him false. The world was not completely upside down. There was a gap in his memory, not an abyss. His position had been that of someone balancing on one foot beside a chasm of unmeasurable immensity. Now he was like a man standing legs spread apart straddling a narrow though deep pit. It was true the pit had to be filled in, but even if it wasn't, he could walk on without the horrible sensation of tottering in pitch darkness along the edge of a cliff.

A sharp weakness seized Craig as he sat there. He swayed, recovered himself, then lay back heavily against the back of the chair. The astounded thought came, "Why, I'm on the point of fainting."

The nausea went away. Carefully, Craig climbed to his feet and filled a glass with water. Back in his chair, he raised the glass to his lips—and saw that his hand was trembling. It startled him. He had, he realized seriously, really let his situation affect him. Thank God, the worst of the purely personal part was over; not entirely over, it was true. But at least he had his beginning established. As soon as his military record arrived he'd be solidly based up to the age of twenty-four. It was a pretty sound base, if you really thought it over. And since his conscious life had resumed at the age of forty-six, that left exactly twenty-two years to be accounted for.

The high confidence drained. Like a settling stone, Craig crouched in his chair. Twenty-two years! His real life-time. Growing up didn't count. That was the animal stage, a sort of enormously prolonged marking time, the preliminary to the main event.

Twenty-two years! Oh, God!—

His military record arrived on the afternoon of the ninth day. It was a printed form, on which the answers were typed in blank spaces provided.

There was his name, his age . . . regiment . . . pre-war occupation—"Clerk". Well, that fitted. There was the name of his next of kin. Serious wounds or injuries: "Amputation of right leg necessitated by injury in fighter plane crash—"

Craig stared. But he still had his right leg, he thought with an owl-like gravity.

The gravity broke like a bomb-shattered dam; and again he stared at the unchanging print. At last he thought: There must be a mistake. Some fool up in the records office had typed the wrong information. Even as one part of his brain developed that argument, another part accepted everything, accepted and knew that there was no mistake, that there was nothing wrong with this form. The wrongness, the mistake, was not there in some government department. It was here in him. He should have known the very instant that he tried to convince himself that he, with his thirty-four-year-old body, was fifty. He had known. The knowledge had been there in his mind like a sick thing fighting against the greatest force in the human ego: the will to have a positive identity. There was no fooling any more. He was not, never had been, Lesley Craig.

Accordingly, the time had come to confront those who knew who he was. Whatever their purpose in impressing upon him the belief that he was Lesley Craig, it must now be forced out into the open.

It was four o'clock by his wrist watch as he turned through the open twenty-foot-high gate, and guided his car along the driveway, in and out among the trees. He drove the machine into the garage. Gregory was there.

Gregory said, "Home early, Mr. Craig."

"Yep!" said Craig.

He walked out through the side door, and along the walk that led to the French windows. He was as calm, he thought, as he'd ever been. There was no reason to be otherwise. He knew exactly what he was going to say and what he wasn't. No side issues. Just his own mental problem, his discovery of the gap in his memory, and the fact that he wasn't Lesley Craig. The rest, the curious rest, didn't matter now. He could go into that later. Now there was only himself.

Anrella was arranging some flowers in the living room. She turned, said serenely, "Why hello there, Les—home early."

In spite of his calmness, there must have been something in his face. Or perhaps—more likely—with her knowledge, she knew what was coming. "Les," she said sharply. "What's the matter?"

Craig felt a brief, unexpected bitterness at the way she was acting it out. Then he said, "Sit down, Anrella. I've got something to tell you."

He began with Nyper's casual remark. He omitted all suggestion that he knew the remark had not been casual, but deliberate. He made no reference to his return home that first day at lunch time and what he had overheard. Clearly, succinctly, he described his discoveries about his own mind.

When he had finished, Anrella said, "Oh, you poor darling. Oh, Les, I'm sorry you've found this out."

Craig saw that she was crying. The tears

shone like jewels in her eyes, and then, no longer gemlike, trickled down her cheeks damply staining the powder that was there. Her eyes remained big and bright and crying.

"It's really very simple, Les. You had a nervous breakdown, a very bad one involving loss of memory; and the present you is a built up personality, painstakingly built up. You mustn't try to tear it down. Let it alone, Les. Forget what you've discovered. Just keep things as they are, for my sake and your own."

"But look here—" Craig began. He left the sentence dangling. Because it could be that. He sat stiffly staring at Anrella fascinated by the explanation. It did explain, up to a point. His mind must have smashed and scattered like a spark struck from metal. Needing then to be refashioned into a coherent wholeness. For an instant, Craig had a mental image of what his mind must have been; an amorphous, groping thing, a blurred picture world, a vast—in a special sense of vastness—formless universe of half memories, of badly wrenched threads of personality, a frayed, tattered, incredible monstrosity of a semi-brain.

It was not a pleasant image to behold, but it braced him. It was the not knowing, he thought, the terrible and increasing uncertainty, that had unnerved him during this past week. Now he knew. The whole thing was resolved down to a simple pattern. He must find out a few more facts, clear his mind of the questions that tormeted it, and then forget the whole matter.

He knew that he would be able to forget. They had done well, those great doctors who had rebuilt his mind. He felt the strength inside him, the boundless strength of a healthy mind that knew its sanity. Yes, they had done well.

His sense of easement faded. He shook himself. Just a minute! Just one minute! What about... and what about... and—

Craig leaned back, laughing inwardly, mirthlessly, at himself. She had nearly got him. But not quite. He stared at Anrella with hard, bright eyes, speculatively. She was probably not the first wife who had lied to her husband with a straight face.

The realization did not make the reality any easier to take.

She was not looking at him. She had taken out her handkerchief and was dabbing at her eyes. She put the handkerchief away finally, and Craig saw that it was time he said something, something that would not give away his disbelief, but which yet would carry on the farce. If he was careful, he might gain some valuable information.

The moment he spoke, however, he recognized that the grim train of his thought was going to be hard to conceal. His voice was sharp, almost harsh, as he said, "But I'm not

Lesley Craig. Lesley Craig is a man fifty years old, who lost a leg in 1944."

She seemed not to notice the strained, unnatural tone of his voice. "Oh, you fool, Les," she said. "Don't you understand? You're a famous medical case. You were found wandering on a roadside without memory, with no knowledge of who you were. You were taken over by doctors of a wealthy foundation, given the identity of a patient who bequeathed his whole property to the foundation while you were there. The reason they gave you an older man's identity was because they wanted you to feel older, to feel more responsible, to feel yourself somebody. I was your nurse, who fell in love with you. Several wealthy men, supporters of the foundation, grew interested in your case, and one of them—Mr. Nesbitt— agreed to give you your present job. Now please don't ask any more questions. I've already told you too much. In fact," she stood up, "I won't say another word until I've talked to Dr. Bovard."

Craig watched her curiously as she walked over to the fireplace. She stood there, head bent, leaning against one of the ornamental protuberances of the mantel. It was disturbing that he could appraise her with such detached coolness. But the astonishing thing was that he was not even bothering to examine her story.

It was a plausible story. He had to admit

that. It actually covered a lot of points that they didn't know he knew, such as the fact that there were wealthy men like Peter Yerd and John Nesbitt in the background of his problem. It wasn't even, Craig decided, that Anrella was doing a poor job of acting. She had cried at the right moment, her voice had held all the right inflections, and the moment of getting up and walking off was a beautifully timed bit of business.

In spite of it all, he didn't believe her. Frankly, utterly, finally, he didn't believe a word she had said. It was hard to put a mental finger on the reasons for his incredulity. There was what he had heard, about their having to go through with something because of Jefferson Dayles.

Craig grimaced hopelessly. Jefferson Dayles. *There* was a meaningless angle to a configuration that was already approaching the obscurity of a four-dimensional object. Beyond question, the story was far from complete. If what she had said was really true, why had they wanted him to know? It was the one method calculated to drive him crazy.

Craig felt the change of color in his face. He thought starkly: *Was that it?* For a moment, then, he fought the terrible suspicion. Because Anrella wouldn't. She wouldn't. Anger came, driving away doubt, flooding, boiling anger that washed caution out of him as if it had never been.

"Why, you incredible scoundrels!" he raged.

He was aware of Anrella turning, staring at him, white-faced. But his rage rode on, gathering force. He shouted, "I overheard what you said last week, do you understand? I listened in on the meeting that was held here nine days ago."

He had intended going on, stabbing at her with his words. But her reaction canceled that.

"You what?" she said in a piercing tone.

Craig was distinctly and amazedly conscious that he had lost the initiative. It was his turn to stare and feel startled. Her face, he saw, was shades whiter under its makeup. Twisted, strained face, distorted eyes. She came toward him with a curiously graceless walk. Her fingers caught his arm; and, like little stones, pressed into his flesh just above the wrist. She said in a caricature of her normal voice:

"What did you hear? *What did you hear?*"

The wildness of her scared him, shocked him. He said uneasily, "Not much. It was too hard to catch the words. But I heard enough to—"

"But you don't know! You don't know the truth?"

The rage was gone out of Craig. There was only impatience with her alarm. "Know what, Anrella!" he snapped. "I assure you, you're in no danger from me."

She seemed not to hear. She let go of his arm, and ran in that graceless way to the phone. Craig watched her stupidly as she dialed a number, and listened thunderstruck as she cried, "Dr. Bovard, come over at once. He heard part of our meeting last week. Yes, yes, he came here to the house—"

She let the phone fall, as if she had forgotten that it had a cradle. On her feet again, she called in a strident voice, "Nickson—Nickson—Nickson—"

"Yes, yes, madam?" The tall, long-faced butler hurried through the alcove from the hall.

"Call Gregory. Tell him to lock the two gates, and put the gardeners to patrolling."

Crazily, the butler ran for the French windows. As the man rushed by, Craig had the impression that Nickson gave him a cool, appraising look. Then he was gone out of the windows. The turmoil was gone with him.

Silence settled. Anrella stood, head drooping, arms limp, near a chair. She looked at the uttermost end of nervous exhaustion. She walked slowly to the chair and slumped into it. She looked up finally, and said in a flat voice:

"I'm sorry, Les. I'm very, very sorry to have to tell you this. But you can't leave the grounds now until"—she stopped, seemed to brace herself, and went on—"until you're completely cured again."

She finished, "You realize, of course, that you are quite mad."

So that was to be the angle.

Chapter
4

He had no plan. He was alone. The tall sapling growing beside the high fence brought the thoughts Suppose this fantastic imprisonment went on and on? Suppose he really wanted to get out of here some day!

Craig started to climb the fence, using the sapling as a brace. Alone, the upper part of the young tree would not have supported him. But by letting the metal poles of the fence carry his weight, and by using the tree as a support only, he reached the top in about three minutes. The speed of his ascent, the easy strength remaining to him, surprised him. It had never occurred to him to assess his physical capacity as anything but "fit."

It was more than that. He hadn't really

needed the tree at all. He balanced himself above the spears of the fence top and looked around him. The fence ran along for about a quarter of a mile in either direction. In the distance beyond a wooded meadowland, he could see the church steeples of the three Alcina churches. Half a dozen planes were circling the town, as if they were searching for something. Trees hid the mansion behind him, and the main gate to the left was barely visible beyond a wavering hedge of mountain ash.

He was alone, briefly his own master. He could leave now, climb or jump down the outer side of the fence, head due west and cross the stream that meandered there, and by that roundabout course cross the countryside toward Alcina. The savings bank would still be open. He had a small account there that he had started on impulse one day when he found himself without funds. He had simply written a cheque on his city bank, deposited it; and he'd never been near the place since. *They* couldn't possibly know about an action like that.

He would be able to leave—but where could he go? Well, there was a train due in about forty-five minutes that would take him to New York. Craig laughed softly, but with bitterness. It was not as easy as that. Physically, perhaps, but not spiritually. A man with his impulses, his instincts, didn't just shoot off to some remote point, and begin life over again.

Damn it all, he was a settled man. He felt settled. Up to a month ago, he had been a happily married business executive, so content with his way of life that even the thought of change had never touched his mind.

There was another thing to remember. Leaving now would seriously diminish his chances of finding out who he was, and what all this was about.

They were waiting for something, or somebody. Craig stiffened with the memory of his analysis of the way, the expectant way they were waiting. Almost every day the moneyed men—Yerd and Nesbitt and Basil Shore and the others—came up, either by train to Alcina, or by car; and they would sit around talking in low tones that ended only when he came into the room, when they became jovial and friendly. But the overshadowing, almost exciting air of waiting for something to happen remained like a miasm of dark hopes.

He, too, must wait, for his own sake. He must know, for his own sake. Besides, there was Anrella!

Clinging with tiring muscles to the metal fence, Craig thought grimly about Anrella. Except for the one astonishing outburst that day he had confronted her, three weeks ago now, she had tried very hard to get their relationship back on its old footing. She had come up behind him one day as he was

57

reading, leaned over and kissed him. He must have scowled at her. She must have considered it a mild reproof. For that night she came to his room. How she cried when he put her out. In the morning he found her sleeping on the rug outside his door. No doubt about it, there was Anrella.

The shaky conviction came to Craig that if she came again, he wouldn't send her away.

After a moment, he glanced wryly along the fence he had climbed. Might as well get down and go back to the house, take another one of the sun baths his body seemed to be craving these days. A man who was having his kind of thoughts wasn't leaving. Not yet.

As he twisted himself gingerly into position for the descent, the planes that had been remote points of thunder, swooped down over his head and skimmed the trees inside the fence. Craig craned his neck, and stared in amazement as they disappeared in the direction of his private landing field. The clattering engines took on the unmistakable, subdued throb of machines in the act of landing. There was the fading-into-silence sound of slowing propellors, then a rattle of smaller engines: Jeeps, Craig recognized with a start. *Jeeps!* Transported by planes. This was an air-borne attack.

And Anrella was at the house. He had been descending frantically before that lashing stream of thought. Now he reached the ground and began to run. He burst out of the brush into an open stretch of meadow, saw the Jeep roaring toward him; and stopped.

Instantly, he whirled and raced for the fence. Fool! He was thinking bitterly. He should have climbed over it in the first place. Men who wanted to save their wives should use a method that might actually save, and not yield to the first wild emotional impulse to fling themselves to the rescue. It was too late now.

The Jeep caught him when he was still twenty feet from the fence. The cool-eyed women who operated it pointed the steadiest pistols Craig had ever faced. A few minutes later, at the house, Craig saw that the whole gang had been rounded up: Anrella, Nesbitt, Yerd, Shore, Cathcott, Gregory, all the servants; altogether forty people were lined up before a regular arsenal of machine guns manned by about a hundred women.

"Les, you're all right?"

Anrella's blue eyes were anxious, her oval face wan and tired as she asked the question.

"Silence!" commanded the deep-voiced woman. But Craig nodded and smiled at Anrella reassuringly.

"That was he all right," reported the leader of the Jeep that had captured him. "I thought I saw somebody on the fence as we were coming in to land. There's a tree there, very close to the fence."

"Cut it down," ordered the deep voice. "And remove other trees that might be used for escape. Put a guard on Lesley Craig night and day; only his wife can be permitted with him. All the others will be removed by plane to Kaggat prison. Action!"

An hour later, Craig was alone with Anrella.

"Darling, what's all this about?"

He felt a dark eagerness as he asked the question. In spite of everything that had happened, by far the most important reality was still the mystery behind this incredible business. What did it all mean? Now, at last, the information could no longer be denied him.

He watched her tensely, where she sat near the window in the great living room. He saw her gaze sweep beyond him to the guards at the doorway, then return and pause on his face. Then she shook her head. Amazingly, she shook her head.

The fury of reaction exploded in his brain. He was dimly aware as he leaped to his feet that the swiftness of his anger showed how raw his nerves had worn during these weeks. He forgot that. In two strides, he reached her chair, loomed over her.

"You've got to tell me," he raged. "How can I even think unless I know more? Don't you see, Anrella—"

He stopped, helpless before her rigid-faced silence. The anger was still there when he spoke again, but controlled memory and purpose were now integral parts of the intricate pattern of his emotions. He said grimly:

"You know, I suppose, that no one but Jefferson Dayles could have sent these women thugs. If you do know that, and know why, tell me, so I can start figuring a way out."

There was a strained look on Anrella's face suddenly. But she did not even glance at him. Craig pressed on, "When I overheard you at the meeting that day, you said something about a change being due. What did that mean? A change in what? In whom? In *me?*"

"It's in you. I won't tell you anything more than that."

He waved a hand at her, as if he was groping through darkness. "You've told me this much, why not tell me more?"

"I haven't told you anything."

Her words stopped him at the edge of a cataclysm of new questions. After a moment, he realized bitterly that she was telling the truth. He still didn't know anything that mattered. His bewilderment was greater than ever. He drew a deep breath, but before he could assail her again, she said:

"The change comes more quickly when you're under strain. You can see yourself how important speed is. That's all I'm going to tell you, Lesley. That's final."

Grimly, Craig stared at her white, determined face. Then with a curt, hard laugh, he whirled and left the room. He was through with her, he thought, utterly through with her.

CHAPTER 5

Craig fingered the rock. He strove so hard for casualness that his hands shook. He grew alarmed, fearful that he might give himself away. He settled closer to the luscious grass on which he sprawled, surrounded by his seven women guards.

The rock was two inches in diameter, two inches of inert stone. Yet it contained in its tiny mass so much of his hope that he trembled in a brief funk. Gradually, however, he quieted down, and settled himself to wait for the boys. Every Saturday since school had started again a month before, he had heard their shrill voices at this time of the morning. The sound came from beyond the thick fringe of trees that hid from his gaze the iron fence which completely surrounded the estate that was his private penitentiary.

The trees and fence separated them from him, and him from all the world. He hadn't dreamed that escape would take so much planning, such an intricate scheme, and two long months of otherwise uneventful waiting. During those months, he'd stopped wondering why no one came from the office to inquire about him; undoubtedly, someone else must be running the firm. He'd completely given up talking to Anrella. She was treating him like a child—an unforgivable action.

It was a bad situation. In minutes now, the boys would be going past here with their fishing rods, heading toward the deep pools farther upstream. And he had no plan to rely on but his own—what was that?

It was, he realized tensely, a sound, a faint vibration of boyish laughter, far away as yet.

But the time had come.

Craig lay still, tautly examining his chances. Two of the women lolled at ease on the ground a dozen feet to his right. Unless they altered their position radically before the moment of action, they would be the least able to interfere with his purpose. Three other women, also in slacks, lounged eight feet to his left, and somewhat behind him. They were too close for comfort, and they looked alert, athletic. One synchronized jump, and they'd bowl him over.

He had no inclination to underestimate them. He did not doubt but that he had been assigned guards strong enough to handle their weight in men. Of the two remaining women, one stood directly behind him at a distance of perhaps eight feet. The other loomed about six feet ahead, directly between him and the tall trees that hid the fence beyond which the boys would be passing. The smoky gray eyes of this powerful creature looked dull and unalert, as if her mind was far away. Craig knew better than that. She was a Jefferson Dayles machine; and she was the most dangerous thing on his horizon.

The medley of sound that preceded the boys was nearer.

Craig felt the throb of his temples, as he reached with a forced deliberateness into his pocket and slowly drew out a glass crystal. He held the little thing in his fingers, letting the rays of the morning sun lance its depths with fire. It blazed as he spun it into the air. As he caught it, snuffing its brilliant light, he was preternaturally conscious of eyes on him, the guards watching him, not with suspicion, but with awareness. Three times Craig flung the glass up several yards into the sky. And then, as if abruptly tiring of the game, threw it to the ground about an arm's length from him. The crystal lay there, glittering in the sun, the brightest object in his vicinity.

He had given much thought to that glass

crystal. It was obvious that no one of the guards could ever maintain a concentrated watch on him. Of the seven, he must assume that three were glancing at him with attention at one moment. When he finally moved, even these would have to look twice, because the reflected flame of the crystal would confuse their gaze and distort their mind pictures of what he was actually doing.

That was the theory—and the boys were nearer.

Their voices rose and fell, a happy babble, now boastful, now in agreement, now one dominating, now all speaking at once. It was impossible even to begin guessing how many there were. But they were there, physical realities, the presences he needed for his plan of escape.

Craig drew the book out of his left-side coat pocket. He opened it idly, not at the place marked but glancing here and there, wasting time, anything to give the women the necessary seconds to adjust their minds to the immensely normal fact that he was going to read. He waited until his nerves shrieked in protest, until his very muscles quivered from the prolonged strain of mummery. And then— he put the book down on the grass with its top edge pressing against the rock.

He opened the book boldly now, at the marker, which was a sheet of notepaper. To the guards, the letter must look exactly like the score of pieces of blank paper he had used in the past two months for taking notes. What was more, it *was* blank.

In spite of his determination to end an intolerable confinement, he actually had nothing to say to any local authorities. Until he knew what was involved in the whole wretched business, the problem was his. Once outside, he could handle it in his own way. He felt curiously, tremendously capable.

There was a stirring to his right. Craig did not look up, but his heart sank clammily. The two women from whom he expected minimum interference were beginning to show life. What damnable luck!

But there could be no delay now. His fingers touched the white missive; perspiring, he shoved it out over the edge of the book, and directly on top of the rock. The sheet, with all its carefully attached elastics, which needed only to be slipped over the little rock to clutch at it with dozens of tiny rubber strands, was quickly attached.

He could not begin to estimate the number of hours he had practiced that synchronized act in the privacy of his room. With a yell— that too was psychology—he lurched to his feet and, with all his strength, flung the stone and its white fluttering cargo.

He had no time to recover his balance or protect himself. Two bodies struck him simultaneously from different angles, flung him ten feet. Craig lay where he fell, dizzy from the blow, but conscious that he wasn't hurt. He heard the leader, the big woman who had been standing in front of him, snapping commands: "Carla, Marion, Jane—back to the house—get Jeeps—cut those kids off from town. Quick! Rhoda, head for the gate, open it for them. Nancy, you and me will climb that fence, and chase after them, or hunt for that letter. Olive, you stay with Mr. Craig."

Craig heard the sound of footsteps as the guards raced off. He waited. Give them time. Give Nancy and the leader opportunity to climb the fence. And then—step two.

At the end of two minutes, he began to groan. He sat up. He saw that the woman was watching him. Olive was a handsome though rather big-boned woman with a thin mouth. She came over.

"Need help, Mr. Craig?"

Mr. Craig! These people with their polite solicitude were enough to drive anybody crazy. Once more he was being illegally imprisoned. Both sides had been equally ruthless there, and equally tender in the administration. The first group, however, had had the best of the tenderness. Up to three months ago, they had included among their kindnesses the fifteen-thousand-a-year job, a loving wife, a home and an estate on a grand style. What could possibly be behind it?

He intended to find out, but in his own way;

not waiting here on somebody else's say-so. And if he was ever going to escape, it had to be now. The trick for getting rid of his guards would not be repeatable. Physically and mentally, Craig stiffened himself. He made a struggle out of climbing onto one knee. Then knelt there, shaking his head as if he were still dazed. He muttered finally, "Give me a hand."

He didn't really count on the woman actually assisting him, although even that was possible in view of their helpful attitude generally.

But she did. She came over and started to bend down. That was when Craig started up. There was no mercy in him in that moment as he struck. These women, with their guns and their ruthlessness, were asking for trouble. A lightning one-two, one-two to the jaw ended the engagement in the first round.

Olive went down like a log. With utter abandon, exactly as if he were attacking a man, Craig plunged on top of her, and rolled her over. In a single synchronized movement, he drew from his pocket the gag he had prepared. It took about a minute to tie it over her flabby mouth.

In a more leisurely fashion now, but without wasted effort, Craig unstuffed his shirt tails, and began to unwind the tough laundry-rope from his waist. As the woman started to squirm weakly, he began his tying-up job.

It required a little over three minutes. He stood up then, shaky but calm. He wasted no further glance on his prisoner, but strode hurriedly off, keeping for a while parallel to the fence. He pushed through the trees finally, scrutinized the territory beyond the fence, and it was as he remembered it: thickly wooded. Satisfied, Craig approached the fence and began to climb. It was like, with some variations, shinnying up a rope.

He reached the top, and, eager now, hitched himself over the spear points of the fence. Afterwards, he realized that he had become too eager.

He slipped.

He made a second mistake, then; the instinctive mistake of trying blindly to save himself. As he fell, one of the spears jabbed his left forearm just below the elbow, and went through. He hung there, his arm skewered to that meat hook of a fence. The pain crashed and roared through his body, and something warm and salty and viscid spurted against his mouth and into his eyes, a choking, blinding horror.

For seconds there was nothing else.

He was lifting himself. That was the first thing Craig knew over and above the tearing agony. Lifting himself with his right arm and, simultaneously, trying to raise his left forearm clear of the dark, clumsy spear that had transfixed it.

Lifting! And succeeding! *Succeeding!* Gibbering, he fell twenty feet to the ground below.

He struck hard. The muscles of his body were pain-clenched cords without give in them. The blow of landing was a bone-jolting smash from the sixty-six million million billion ton battering ram that was Earth. His brain joggled in its cranium. He fell to his knees, then got up again like an animal, with only one impulse left to its shattered body. Get away! Get out of here. They'd be coming, searching. Get out! Get going!

No other consciousness touched Craig until he reached the stream. The water was warm, but it was a late-October warmth. It soothed his burning lips; it brought sanity back to his feverish eyes. He washed his face, then struggled out of the left sleeve of his coat and soaked and washed his arm. The water turned red. The blood welled and bubbled from a wound so gaping and terrible that he swayed and just in time flung himself backwards onto the grassy bank.

How long he lay there, he had no conception; but he thought finally, "Tourniquet, or die!" With an effort of will as much as strength he tore the damp and bloody shirt sleeve at the shoulder, and wound it around and around the upper part of his arm. He twisted it tight with a short, broken end of tree branch, so tight that it hurt his muscles. His arm began to tingle, a not unpleasant tingle. The bleeding stopped.

He staggered to his feet, and began to follow

the stream. That had been his original intention, and now his body remembered. It was easier to follow a previously chosen route than to think out a new one. Time passed. Just when the idea came that it wouldn't do to go straight to the savings bank, he had no conception. There was a vague memory of meeting someone and saying:

"Hurt my arm! Where does the nearest doctor live?"

There must have been an answer. Because after another lapse of inestimable time he was walking along a street thinly overhung with autumn foliage. He realized at intervals that he was looking for a plaque with a name on it. All feeling was long since gone out of his arm. It hung down, swinging as he walked, but it was the lifeless sway of an inanimate object.

He grew weaker, and weariness lay on him like a terrible weight. He kept touching the tourniquet to make sure it wasn't loosening and permitting the blood that still remained to him to seep out. Then he was climbing steps on his knees.

"Christmas!" a man's voice said. "What's this?"

There was a gap, through which a voice penetrated at intervals; then he was in an automobile, with that same voice waxing and waning in his ears.

"You incredible fool, whoever you are.

You've had that tourniquet on an hour at least. Didn't you know—tourniquets must be loosened every fifteen minutes—to let the blood flow—arm must have more blood to stay alive. Nothing now but amputate!"

CHAPTER
6

Craig awakened with a start, and stared dully at the stump of his arm. His whole shoulder was raised on some kind of a netted sling; and the arm was bare and plainly visible. An infrared lamp was pouring its heat on it, and the remnant felt cosy and comfortable, not at all painful.

It was not bleeding; and there was a growth from it, a curled, pink, fleshy thing that seemed like some torn part of the shattered arm, which for some reason had not been cut off.

Then he saw that it had a shape. He stared and stared; and there was a memory in him of a military record that had read: "Amputation of leg necessitated by—"

He slept.

Far away, a man's voice was saying, "There's no longer any doubt. It's a new arm growing in place of the torn-off one. We've been doing a little surgical work—though, as I said to Pentry, I'm hanged if I don't believe the growth is basically so healthy that it could get along without medical attention. It'll be several days before he regains consciousness. Shock, you know."

The voice faded, then came back:

"Toti-potent...toti-potent cells. We've always known, of course, that every human cell has latent in it the form of the whole body; somewhere in the remote past the body apparently took the easiest course of simply repairing damaged tissues."

There was a pause. Craig had the distinct impression that someone was rubbing his hands together in satisfaction. A second man's voice murmured something inaudible, then the first voice went resonantly on, "No clue yet to his identity. Dr. Philipson, who brought him here, never saw him before. Of course, a lot of people from both Big Town and Middle City live all through the Alcina district but...no, we're not giving out any publicity. We want to watch further developments in that arm first. Yes, I'll phone you."

The murmuring, second voice said something, and then there was the sound of a door closing.

He'd have to tell them, Craig thought. He'd have to tell these doctors, as soon as he felt a little less drowsy, about the imprisonment. Anrella had to be freed.

They *knew*, Anrella and the others, though why they hadn't told him—and why they had taken all those precautions! The tense emotion dimmed. What was it Anrella had said that first noon when he had overheard her speaking to the others, about the time for the change having come?

This change! It must be a periodic transformation inside him. It must have happened before. But why hadn't they told him? Why?

Sleep came like a soothing blanket of forgetfulness.

"Try!" the man was saying. "Try to remember!"

A trickle of sweat sagged down Craig's face. All through his lean, strong body he felt the gathering tension of enormous effort, and there was a sudden high pain in his arm. In the vaguest way, he was aware of the white-starched figure of his nurse, and of another nurse sitting with pencil poised over a notebook, and of the dark night beyond the window.

He gritted the pain out of his mind; and, with the whole strength of that mind, strained to penetrate the mesh of waver and blur that lay like a cloud over his memory. Pictures took vague shape there, formless thoughts and shadow memories of days unutterly dim. It was not memory but memory of memory. He was isolated in a little island of impressions of the moment, and the terrible sea of blankness all around was sweeping closer, pushing harder every minute, every second.

With a gasp, he let the pressure of strength and strain slacken inside him. He stared helplessly at the doctor. "Useless," he said simply. "My name, I think, is...is—" He stopped, and shook himself. "I can't remember. There's something about an iron fence and—what city is this? Maybe that will help."

"Middle City," said the doctor. His brown eyes watched Craig narrowly. But the latter shook his head.

"What about Big Town?" the doctor asked. "That's a city about forty miles from here. Dr. Philipson brought you to Middle City from Alcina because he knows the hospitals here." He repeated it slowly: "Big Town!"

For a moment there seemed to be a fuzzy familiarity. And then Craig shook his head. He stopped the weary movement as an idea struck him. "Doctor, how is it that I can use the language, when everything else is so dim?"

The man stared at him unsmiling, grim, "You won't be able to speak in a few days unless you spend every spare minute reading and talking just to keep those particular conditioned reflexes alive."

He was aware of the doctor half-turning from him, facing the two nurses. "I want a detailed, typewritten account prepared for the patient, giving the complete story of his case as far as we know it. Have a radio brought in here, and"—he turned back to the bed, smiling darkly—"you keep it on. Listen to the soap operas, if no one else is talking. When you're not listening or sleeping, read, read aloud."

"What if I don't?" His lips were ash-dry. "Why do I have to do this?"

The doctor's voice was grave. "Because, if you don't your brain will become almost as blank as a new born baby's. There may be"—he hesitated—"other reactions, but we don't know that. We do know that you are forgetting your past at an alarming rate. The reason for that is that ordinarily the cells in the human body and brain are in a continuous state of being used and being repaired. Every hour, every day, your billions of memory cells are undergoing that repair; and apparently, in the mending, the little wave of memory electrically stored away is not damaged, at least, not seriously damaged. In the long run, no doubt, the replacement of tissue diminishes the store of memory. Perhaps there lies the true explanation of why memories grow dimmer with the years. Now, with you, it's different. You have at this instant toti-potent cells. Instead of being repaired, your cells have been replaced by brand new, healthy cells; and those new cells know nothing of the memory carried by the old, for memory is not hereditary. You have cells as potentially capable of storing memory as your old ones, but all you can store in them before they in turn are replaced will be the impressions gained by your mind in a period of, say, a week, perhaps a little longer."

The doctor finished briskly: "Your name, for the record, will be Peter Smith. Try to remember that, will you?"

He examined the name mentally: "Smith!" he said finally, aloud. He lay, listening to the rhythm of it go through his mind, then repeated: "Peter Smith."

"That's right," said the doctor. "Now, any questions?"

"Yes. Why not take me to the town of Alcina? I have a conviction"—Smith paused, and a tenseness welled up inside of him— "that it's very important."

"Impossible!" The doctor spoke sharply. "I assure you we are doing all we can to identify you. Tomorrow's issue of the Alcina Weekly Herald will contain a story about you. But you can't leave here now. Your arm was amputated only thirteen days ago!"

"But I feel all right."

He saw that the argument was useless. He lay back. The doctor said, "Just rest yourself. And do as I've said."

There was a sound at the door. An interne

looked in. "Thought you might be interested," he said. "The word was just flashed on the radio. Jefferson Dayles is re-elected president by a majority of two million."

"Thank God!" said the doctor, sighing. "I felt sure neurotic America would elect that woman. I have no doubt she's intellectually capable, and could handle the job. But it's too fast, a passing whim of an unstable electorate. Reaction would be just as swift, and could easily destroy all the built-up progress of the last two centuries. Women must take over their share of political power gradually, not in one emotional spree."

"Oh, you men!" said one of the nurses in quiet fury.

The second nurse snapped, "Don't forget it was only two million majority. Next time—"

They went out. The silence of night settled. Twice, as he lay there, footsteps moved along the hallway, grew loud, and receded into distance. He lay quiet, completely awake.

He thought, "Have to get to Alcina. Can't wait!"

He climbed out of bed. There was no sense of pain or dizziness. It did not occur to him that he was not dressed for outdoors. He knew better, though, than to leave by the door.

The window was hard to open. He found a metal fence beyond, and a narrow staircase leading down. He went down into the strange world of night. A chill wind was blowing, but the warmth of the bed was still in him, and the discomfort seemed unimportant. His bare feet began to hurt after he reached the ground, from the roughness that he kept stepping on. But he pressed forward grimly until he came to a hard, smooth surface.

Two lights in the distance of that dim-lit street attracted his attention, because they moved. And they made a roaring sound. The lights and the sound fascinated him. Intrigued, he stepped toward them out of the shadow of a tree. In a flash they were upon him. At the last instant, he saw that behind the lights was a large, black shape.

There was an unimaginably hard blow, then a faraway squealing sound, then distant voices, "We're drunk, all of us. Nobody'll believe he stepped into our path. It's jail for sure. Quick, get him into the car, then first to Ned's place to get some more gas, then we'll dump the body a hundred miles from here. Hell, we've got to do it. We can't afford—"

For a week, the thing that had been Lesley Craig lay in a ditch, very still, re-growing!

CHAPTER
7

Jefferson Dayles studied the report of the
scientists on the eve of inauguration. The first
perusal left him blankly puzzled. Later, he
thought, later when the excitement was over
he would read it more carefully. But he took it
to bed with him, and in the middle of the night
rose and re-read sketchily the astounding
document.

> In the matter of two so-called elec-
> tric-engined automobiles and the so-
> called electric-engined plane turned
> over to us by your agents...
> Electronic-engined would have
> been a better term. The motive power
> seems to be derived from a dark metal

electronic tube which, when taken apart, proved too intricate for reassembly, in spite of all our careful notations on each phase of the process. (The suggestion has been made that this "tube" was drawing power from a distant power broadcasting station.)

As the failure resulted in spite of the fact that we took apart, not one, but two of the engines, we have determined not to dismantle the third and last engine until after a very careful and, we recommend in the event others are assigned to the investigation, a very exhaustive study of the parts of the two tubes already dismembered.

It is possible the secret of their reaction may lie in some subtle alloy combination of the construction materials. Even the welding compound must be examined and analyed for its possible influence...

The surpassing importance of cautious development can best be gauged by our discovery that the power has other potentialties about which a report is being prepared.

Jefferson Dayles crawled back into bed, and lay in the darkness with closed eyes thinking: It was the old, old story: Too complicated for mortal minds.

As he took the oath for his second term, Jefferson Dayles thought: Three years, and no more. Three years to find him.

After that it might be too late.

Too late, too late—all that great day the words trampled through his mind, dulling his smiles, dimming his exultation, darkening all his thought. Find Craig! Find the man whose blood could in one week strip the old age from his body, and, in so doing, immortalize his power and the mighty civilization he visualized.

The thought was like a sickness, a craving, that was still upon him six months later when they brought in the farmer. The man was big and rangy. As he sat listening to the fellow's extremely colloquial account, one question quivered in Jefferson Dayles' mind. The problem of how to phrase it engaged his attention as the farmer's voice twanged on:

"...Like I was sayin', he was at my place ten days, an' old Doc Gillespie came twicet to look at him, but he didn't seem to need no medical attention, only food. Mind you, he did act queer. Wouldn't tell me his name or nuthin'. Anyways, I finally took him to Carness and turned him over to the employment commission. I told the fellow in charge that his name was Bill Smith. He didn't argue none about that, so that's what they put him down as—Bill Smith. There was some labor job they sent him to, can't just recollect what it was. Anything else you wanta know?"

Jefferson Dayles sat cold. But that was an outward covering for an inner excitement. Craig was alive. Discovered, so Kay had said, when an old news item was followed up, a news item which reported that on November 21, 1972, somebody had called the police department of the nearby city of Carness and reported a body in a roadside ditch.

Actually, this farmer had already found Craig when the phone call was received. So it was obvious that the person making the call must have been one of those responsible for leaving Craig in that icy gutter. Somebody became conscience-stricken, or perhaps simply anxious to get the whole affair over and forgotten. The exact psychology of it didn't matter.

The toti-potent man was alive.

There was one question that remained, a verification: Craig's arm! The one that had been re-growing. The farmer's voice came again:

"There's one more thing, Mr. President—"

Jefferson Dayles waited, involved in the preparation of his question. It was a hard sentence to utter because, well, you couldn't ask if a human being's arm had regrown. You couldn't, although the very idea was fascinating and mind-staggering.

"The thing," said the farmer, "is this: when I picked him up, I coulda swore one o' his arms was shorter'n t'other. Yet when he left, they wuz the same length. Now, am I crazy or—"

"Doesn't make much sense, does it?" said Jefferson Dayles. He went on quietly, "Thank you for your assistance. My secretary will see to it that you are well paid for your trouble. You will, I hope, continue to regard silence about this interview as a duty to your country."

"You kin count on me," said the man with the quiet positivity of sublime and unquestioning patriotism. "An' you kin forget about the money."

But Jefferson Dayles had his own conscience to assuage. He mustered a smile. "No," he said, "we mustn't forget money. It's a valuable aid to good living, so I've been told."

As a clerk Prowse rather fancied himself. He spent a large part of his money on clothes, and, in the beginning, he was always hurrying up and down the long aisles of the Workman's Compensation Board offices, past the men who were really working, and not simply pretending.

Neat, natty little man, he nursed a tiny, obstinate mustache, and an attitude of coarse humor towards his superiors. They must have thought it showed an adult trend of mind for in seven years, which was literally no time at all in such a dead level organization, he was chief of one section of the filing department, a sharp-tongued, fault-finding straw boss. Ossification of the brain set in at the ripe age of thirty-one, and his ephemerally youthful body began to dry up. At thirty-five, he was a little bespectacled runt with cold blue, suspicious eyes and a hatred of the world that, though he couldn't figure out just how it had happened, had mistreated him.

To his desk in December, 1973, were brought two files under the names of Bill Smith and William Smith. Bill, according to the statements in the document, had had his left arm cut off at the elbow. And William had lost the fingers of his left hand at a somewhat later date. In both cases compensation was being paid at the full allowable rates, but that was only incidentally important. What interested Prowse was that Bill and William Smith both lived at Apartment N, 111 Hunt Street.

"Shall I combine the two files?" said the wan-voiced female slave who had discovered the similarity.

"Leave them on my desk," replied the pontiff.

He meditated over the problem during the next half hour. If the fingers had been lost *before* the forearm, the identification would have been simpler. But they hadn't. And there was the doctor's signatures and all other necessary data.

It was a situation requiring all the curious and complicated skills of the head of a filing department, requiring moreover, a decision. Frowning, Prowse studied not only the files but the index cards in the cabinets. There were eleven blocks of "Smith" cards; and among them he found five other cards, one of them under the name of Bill. The others were, in alphabetical order, Frank, George, Milton and Tom. The seven Smiths possessed among other common denominators, according to their files, the fact that they all lived at Apartment N, 111 Hunt Street.

The new Bill had lost his right hand. Frank Smith had suffered severe head and shoulder injuries. George's face had been smashed. Milton and Tom had each lost a left arm. In every case the name of the wife was given as Gracie Smith, and it was to her that the checks for compensation were made out.

"Naturally," Prowse finished his story to President Dayles, "we had him arrested."

He shook his head wonderingly. "He was a pretty smart chap, that fellow Smith. The woman had skipped with the money; and Smith just played dumb at the trial, never saying a word. Because of our inability to prove how it had been done the judge gave him only six months. He got out," Prowse finished, "four months ago."

Four months. It turned out to be four months too long. The trail ended at the prison gate. A guard recalled that a car had been waiting for Craig. It drove off into the oblivion of the vast land that was the United States.

Women won two-thirds of the contested seats in the mid-term elections. And went mad with hope. By the end of November every city had its daily parade, its line of sullen men watching, and other men cheering.

Jefferson Dayles had allowed the election to be honest because he was genuinely anxious to learn the exact situation and because of the sobering effect power might have.

"Women," he told Kay, "might as well discover before it's too late that politics are a painful business for the physically weak. Men have fought to an uneasy balance, which has made for a false atmosphere of quiet and dignity. I firmly expect that the men who are now such ardent supporters of women in Congress will be in time their most violent enemies."

He smiled with savage sardonicism. "Prepare the hospitals," he said, "for women with broken heads, and the jails for men who break them—and find Craig, or we'll be swamped by a sea of emotionalism."

The year ground heavily towards its end— and didn't quite make it unscathed. On Christmas Eve, press wires hummed, radios broke off programs to announce: Los Angeles—A long line of women marching with placards—"HURRAH FOR THE

89

RIGHTS OF WOMEN" "IN THE WORLD OF THE FUTURE MEN WILL DO THE PHYSICAL WORK WOMEN THE ADMINISTRATIVE" "A JUST ORDERLY PEACEFUL WORLD ADMINISTERED BY WOMEN—"

A man's interrupting shout: "Break it up, let's break it up! They're counting on us to respect them, while they make slaves of us. Come on!"

Men surged sullenly from the sidelines, and became a mob. When armored cars finally cleared the streets, twenty-four women lay dead, ninety-seven others were seriously injured, and more than four hundred required hospital treatment.

The pathological nature of the assault was revealed when four of the men accused of murder proved with the assistance of lie detectors that they had voted for women in the elections. They were unable to account for their violent change of heart, except for one who stated plaintively that he suddenly "saw that there would be hell to pay if women ever really got into power."

Three days before the date set for their execution, all of the seventeen men condemned for the parade killings staged a mass escape from the death house.

There were riots in a dozen cities, and mass delegations of women demanded punishment for the prison guards responsible, and that the escaped men be immediately recaptured and gassed.

It was a crisis of the kind that could win or lose five million votes; and Jefferson Dayles made a speech to the nation, promising all possible action would be taken.

On the second day following his speech, the letter arrived, the letter which read:

> Cell 676, Kaggat Prison,
> January 27, 1975.

Dear Mr. President:

> I have learned that my husband was one of the seventeen condemned men, and I know where he and they are. Speed is essential if his life is to be saved. Please hurry.
>
> Anrella Craig.

The cell did not look as comfortable as he had originally ordered it should be. Jefferson Dayles made a mental note to deliver a sharp reprimand on the matter, then turned his attention to the pale creature that was Anrella Craig.

It was his first face-to-face contact. And in spite of her bleached appearance, he felt impressed. There was something about her eyes, a dignity and power, a maturity that was disturbing. After that first impression, the dullness of her voice surprised him. She sounded more beaten than she looked. Anrella Craig said:

"No, I *want* to tell you. Lesley is in hiding in the great California desert. The ranch is located about forty miles north of the village of Mountainside—" She broke off. "Please don't ask me under what circumstances he did what he did. The important thing is to make sure when you find the hideout that he is not killed." She smiled wanly. "Our original belief was that, as a group, we could through him dominate world affairs. I'm afraid we over-estimated our capabilities."

On the north-bound plane, Kay said: "I see no reason why either Mrs. Craig or any of the others should be released. Now that she has so foolishly revealed her ace in the hole, Craig's identity as one of the parade killers, we owe her nothing."

There was an interruption. "A radiogram message, Mr. President, from Kaggat prison."

Jefferson Dayles read the long message with pursed lips, then handed it without a word to Kay.

"Escaped!" Kay cried. "The whole gang!" She sat very still. "Why, the little, white-faced actress, standing there pretending to be depressed to the point of nothing-else-matters-but-that-he-be-saved. But why did she tell us? Why—"

She stopped, and re-read the message, and whispered finally, "Did you see this? Ninety planes participated in the rescue. What an organization they must have. It means the escape could have been managed at any time. And yet they waited until now. Sir, this is very serious."

Jefferson Dayles felt curiously remote from his assistant's half panic. His mood was exhilaration, and there was in him an intense and gathering will to victory. The situation was indeed serious; here, in fact, was the crisis. His voice lashed out a staccato of orders:

"Kay, you will take personal charge. Use at least five divisions, at least two of them armored, and as many planes as you need, not ninety, but nine hundred. Surround the desert. Check all traffic on land or in the air moving out of it. Use radar detectors at night, searchlights, night fighters. I give you unlimited power to use all the available forces of the United States. Capture Craig!"

He was, he realized, literally fighting for *life*.

CHAPTER
8

Craig awakened. It wasn't anything to think about. Where there had been blackness was suddenly light. He lay very still. He had no consciousness that he had a name, or that there was anything unusual about the situation. *He* was here—the entity that was himself—lying down. Even the posture seemed normal, the very essence of life as it was lived. He was lying down, and aware of himself.

For a long, long time that was all there was. He had no purpose other than being where he was, no memory of anything else, not the faintest conception of movement. He lay, and he stared up at a ceiling that was light-blue in color. It was not the brightest region in his universe and so, after a while, his eyes were drawn to the window through which light blazed dazzlingly.

Like a child absorbed by shiningness, he brought up his arm, and reached towards the window. The intervening emptiness rebuffed him. Instantly that didn't matter, because he became interested in his groping arm. He did realize that the arm was part of himself. The moment he ceased his instinctive reaching, the muscles that supported the arm in the air began to relax. The arm collapsed onto the bed. And because his gaze had followed its clumsy fall, for the first time he grew aware of the bed. He was still examining it, half sitting up the better to look at it, when the sound of footsteps intruded upon his attention.

The sound came nearer, but he did not wonder about it. It was there in his ears, as normal as everything else. The difference was, he was suddenly mentally divided into two sections. One part remained in the bed. The other stared out at the world through the eyes of a man who was coming through an adjoining room towards the door of the bedroom.

He knew the other entity was a man, and that the room-door and act of walking were what they were because, to the second part of his mind, those facts were casual realities of life. The second mind was aware of other things too; and so rapid, so completely absorbent was his own brain that, as the door opened, he swung his legs off the bed, and said:

"Bring my clothes, will you, Peters?"

Peters' brain took the impact of the demand with complete acquiescence. He went out, and there was a satisfying mind picture of him fumbling in a clothes closet. He came back, and paused just inside the door, blinking with new thought. He was a little man in shirt sleeves, carrying a lot of clothing. And he peered over them, and said owlishly:

"Lordy, Bill, you can't get up yet. You were still unconscious half an hour ago when we caught that dame in here." He broke off solicitously: "I'll call the doc and bring you some hot soup. After the way you got us out of the death house, we're taking no chances of anything going wrong with you. Lie back, will you?" -

Craig, watching the other lay the clothes on a chair, hesitated. The argument seemed reasonable, yet somehow not quite applicable to him. After a moment he still hadn't put a mental finger on the flaw. His hesitation ended. He drew his legs back under the quilt, and said:

"Maybe you've got something there. But the way that woman was captured right in this room started me worrying about our hideout here."

He stopped, with a frown. Flashing insight

came that he hadn't been worried until Peters appeared on the scene, and that in fact his mental state at the beginning had been—what?

The memory galvanized his thought. His mind twisted back to the moment of his regaining consciousness. It was amazingly hard to picture himself as he had been at that first instant, blank-brained, without memory. And then instantly absorbing the entire mind of Peters, with all Peters' fears and emotional immaturities. What was utterly astounding was that his memory took in Peters' mind and Peters' knowledge. But nothing else. Nothing of himself.

He stared at the man. That profound but swift examination took in all Peters' memory, and went back through the simple career of a chunky boy who wanted to be a mechanic. No particular reason existed why Peters should have joined the mob that attacked the parade of women. And the actual mob scene was blurred, the trial that followed a nightmare of twisting thought forms dominated by fears so terrible that not a single image came clear. The fear had faded into excited hope during the escape; and so there was a reasonably detailed remembrance of exactly how the prison break had been worked three days before the date set for the mass hanging.

"Did I really do all that?" Craig thought incredulously.

After a moment the fact was still there, a rigid part of Peters' memory of the event. He had taken apart the radio in his cell and, with the addition of parts from radios handed to him from other cells, had manufactured a very pale white light that ate through concrete and steel as if they were insubstantial matter. A guard confronting them had screamed as his gun dissolved in his hands, his clothes disintegrated from his body. The scream must have been pure hysteria, because that pale, intense fire had not harmed him.

The very nature of the weapon, and the mode of exit it provided, prevented the reinforcements brought by the scream from being effective. The police didn't think of solid walls being breached. The cars were at the arranged rendezvous, and the planes, each with its pilot, were concealed beside the grass field across which they took off.

All this was in Peters' memory, as well as the fact that the man known as Bill Smith had been hit by a machinegun bullet as the cars raced away from the prison—the only casualty—carefully looked after. For ten days he had lain unconscious.

Craig pondered about it while Peters went for the soup. He decided, finally, that he was different. It needed only the simplest reflection to realize that reading thoughts, actually absorbing another's mind, was unheard of in Peters' lexicon of life.

He was slowly sipping his soup when Doc McLarg came in. Seen face to face, and not merely as a memory image of Peters' transferred mind. the doctor was a spare-built man about thirty-five and possessed of shrewd brown eyes. The history behind that physical exterior was more complicated than that of Peters, but the relevant facts were simple. A public health officer, McLarg had been forced to resign because of careless work, and was replaced by a woman doctor. On Christmas Eve, in an advanced state of poverty and drunkenness, he had joined lustily in the attack on the parading women.

His examination was that of a nonplussed man. "It's beyond me," he confessed finally. "Ten days ago, I cut a machine-gun bullet out of your chest, and for three days now there hasn't been either an entrance or exit wound. If I didn't know it was impossible, I'd guess you were perfectly well."

There seemed nothing to say to that. McLarg's mind had slipped so gently into his, its knowledge so easily and naturally integrated with that derived from Peters that, even now it was hard to grasp that the information hadn't been there all the time.

He thought about the woman later, frowningly. She had been in his room, bending over him. She had just walked in, she had said. Walked in unseen—into a den of alert, hunted outlaws!

It seemed ridiculous. Uncertain what to do with her, the men had finally locked her in one of the spare rooms of the hacienda. It was odd that, though the house blurred and wavered with thoughts as men went tensely to and fro, hers was not among them. Not once did he catch even a tendril of mind stuff that might belong to a woman. Surely a woman's thoughts would be unmistakable.

Sleep found Craig still puzzling over the whole problem of her.

CHAPTER
9

He awakened with a start in pitch darkness, conscious that there was someone in the room.

"Quiet!" the woman's voice whispered in his ear. "This is a gun."

The paralyzing thing was that he couldn't catch a glimmer of her thought. His mind leaped to his earlier speculation on the subject, and then to a simple conclusion: *He couldn't read the minds of women!*

"Huh!" he began blankly, "what—"

In the darkness he felt the metal pressing against his head, and his thought suffered a dreadful pause. The woman spoke again:

"Take your clothes—never mind dressing—and walk slowly to the door of your clothes closet. There is an open panel inside with steps leading down. Go down them!"

In a sweat of mental agony, he fumbled for his clothes. He was thinking: How could she have escaped from her room?

"I wish," he whispered hoarsely, "the others had killed you instead of just arguing about it, you—"

He stopped, because the gun was pressing against the back of his pajama coat, urging him along.

"Quiet!" came the peremptory whisper. "The truth is, Lesley, you're to be given a few facts about yourself before the authorities close in, as they will do very shortly. Now, please hurry."

"What did you call me?"

"Move!"

He walked slowly, but his mind was like a clenched fist, tightening around the tremendous reality that was here. She knew him. This woman they had captured, this—what had she said her name was?—Anrella Craig *knew* his real identity.

He had had a vague plan of whirling on her in the darkness and grabbing her gun. But that was shattered by her words.

He had to squeeze through the panel; it was so narrow. The staircase was a winding affair that led steeply downward. After the first full turns, a series of tiny costobulbs began. Their misty ray made the passageway seem more alive, more real. For the first time, the fact of them made an impact on his brain. Here was an old ranchhouse to which seventeen condemned murderers had fled turning out to be honey-combed with secret panels. It couldn't possibly be an accident.

One swift grab at her legs, he decided.

"Lesley!" Her voice was a sigh from behind him. "I swear that this will not add one iota to the danger you are all in. When you consider that it is our organization that placed those cars and planes at your disposal when you escaped from prison, you—"

"What?" He stopped, protested, "Listen, those cars and planes were given us by the friend of—"

"An individual giving four cars and two planes. Don't be silly."

"But—"

He broke off, fascinated by her logic; then, "You keep calling me Lesley. Lesley what?"

"Lesley Craig."

"But your name is Anrella Craig."

"That's right. You're my husband. Now, move down those steps."

"If you're my wife," Craig flashed, "you'll prove it by giving me the gun, and trusting me. Give it to me."

The weapon was thrust so quickly past his shoulder that he blinked at it, then reached for it gingerly, half expecting it to be withdrawn.

It wasn't. His fingers closed over it, hers released it. He stood with the gun, nonplussed by the easy victory, feeling stripped of all possibilities of violence.

"Please go down," her voice came.

"But who is Lesley Craig?"

"You will know in a few minutes. Now, please."

He went. Down, down, down. Twice they passed solid steel plates that pressed out to every wall of the staircase, like floors of protective battleship deck metal. The thickness of them made Craig stare. Eight inches. *Each!*

Here was a fortress.

The end came suddenly. A narrow corridor, a door, and then a blaze of lights, a great room filled with machines. There were doors leading to other rooms, tantalizing glimpses of gleaming staircases that went down—tantalizing because they suggested other great tiers of rooms below. The weight began to lift from his mind; the weight of conviction that had lain all afternoon on his brain and body, the conviction that he and Peters and the others had no chance of escape. Here, in this subterranean world, was safety!

His brain squeezed out of its prison of depression. It began to work faster. He felt the surge of new life. It was a sudden abnormal alertness, a glow diffusing his whole being. His gaze flashed the rounds of the machine room, questioningly. His mind strained to locate signs of human occupancy. He had time to notice keenly that even the thoughts of Peters and the others did not penetrate into these metallically sealed depths.

A door opened in the wall to his right; three men emerged. The physical act of emergence scarcely mattered. At the very instant of the door opening, their thoughts, their minds, darted out to him.

It was a veritable flood of thoughts about himself, his past, his *life*. Through that turmoil of impression, Craig heard one of the men whisper to the woman.

"Any trouble?"

"None. All the elaborate precautions were unnecessary. Their search was cursory in the extreme. They did talk half-heartedly about killing me, but I could have frustrated that at any time. Not once did anyone suggest examining the buttons of my clothes for secret gases...but *sssh* now, let him get what's in your minds without interruption."

The man's voice said, "He's getting it all right."

The picture that came was limited in time. It began around the time that Nypers had first hinted to him something was wrong. It showed him being picked up by an old farmer from the ditch where he had been tossed. Who had tossed him there was not clear, because they hadn't located him until a week later. From that point on, however, he had never been out of their sight, although not once, until he was released from jail after being convicted of violating the Workman's Compensation Act, had they interfered in his life. They had not even protected him from the amoral woman who had collected the compensation for his injuries.

They had taken him finally, however, to one of their headquarters. Immediately after the parade killings had rushed him to Los Angeles where they faked photographs implicating him in the attack. And they had a deadly plan.

Craig broke the silence in a strained, astounded voice, "Am I to understand that Peters, McLarg and I, Kelger, Rainey and the others, are going to be kept up there on the surface while the United States army and air force tries to capture us? And you're going to stand by and watch us try to figure a way out, but do nothing to help us?"

He saw that his—wife—was nodding coolly.

Her eyes were bright and oddly sympathetic. "You're in the spotlight, Lesley. You've got to do even better than when you escaped from the jail. You've got to lift yourself almost literally by your mental bootstraps, and become a superman. You see, you're in the final phase of your final change. Whatever you raise yourself to now will be permanent. No more changes. You either become like the rest of us toti-potents or—"

Her eyes lighted. Her hands reached forward impulsively and caught his arm. "Lesley, don't you see? *Don't you see!* We owed it to you; we owed it to the poor, beaten, hopeless world, to give you this chance. Come over here and sit down. I must tell you in a few words. I must persuade you."

She tugged at him. And after a moment's hesitation, Craig allowed himself to be led towards a chair. Her voice was a melodious sound-force that beat at him. "I'm going up there with you. None of us will survive if you fail. That we resolved long ago. Lesley, here below ground is a marvelous machine shop. In a few minutes the greatest male scientists in our organization will be brought in one by one—and you can take their minds, their massive knowledge, and make it your own. I'm sorry you can't read the minds of women, because we have some wonderful women scientists. The whole of our Martian organization is built around the invention of Martha Eger—"

"Your *what* organization?" Craig gasped.

She seemed not to hear. She sat before him on the floor, looking up at him with eyes that were jewel bright and misty with the beginning of tears.

"Lesley, the world is a rotten mess. The United States has never recovered from the cold war that followed World War II. Individual and national moralities are delicate structures capable of withstanding great strains, but easily warped. Every time a rich man's son or a nobleman's heir gain special advantages because of their birth, less favored individuals everywhere shrink a little deeper into their inferiority complexes, seek a little harder for escape from the destroying realities around them. That, of course, is minor. People are too busy for the most part to be aware of what they are reacting to. But in a parallel and greater fashion nations which have shed enormous quantities of blood for a cause that somehow fails to win out are drained of strength. Cynicism breeds too easily, moralities collapse in an astounding way. Weeds grow easily where flowers bloomed a single season before.

"Human science, so marvelously adaptive during the war, never recovered from the restrictions of the cold war. The whole earth stagnates today in a negative futility of ten thousand purposes, all of them doomed to frustration because there is no clear, unifying thread running through them. Jefferson Dayles' analysis of the world and the local situation is quite accurate. Men will vote women into power once. Within a few months they will want to plunge them back into a state of semiservility far worse than anything prevailing now. The trouble is that women are demanding extreme power. Always it is the extremists who dominate, without any great resistance from those who follow them.

"Oh, I admit *we* have done things. But man must work out his own destiny. Nothing in all human history is truer than that the race from which we have sprung cannot survive if, for instance, we furnish them with new inventions and our great science. We're a backwater, an accident. The thirty-five of us—that includes you—can furnish a quart of blood every few months to people of our blood type, and so give them youth, and so tie them to us with inhumanly strong bonds because at the end of thirty years they must again have the blood, or they die normally.

"Each of us can thus give temporary immortality to some three hundred people. But it ends there. The rest of the human race is excluded. Altogether, eighteen children have been born to the twenty women among us. One child was yours and mine, but it and the others had only a slightly greater toti-potent tendency than the average human being. Two gruesome experiments convinced us that toti-potency is not hereditary. So you see, we don't belong to the main stream of human struggle.

"But that doesn't mean we shouldn't try to help them, particularly when you consider that even the thirty-four failures among us have at least twice the average human brain capacity. Twenty times is possible. We know it is possible because some of us attained a great degree of it during those gray, unremembered months that make up a toti-potent period.

"Listen, here, is my story, my little bit of evidence. I was born in 1896, became a nurse in the First World War, and had my right arm torn off by a high explosive shell. It must have been the mud that saved me from bleeding to death. For days I lay untended; and note this well: There is no record of anyone becoming toti-potent without such sustained pressure on them. A body given prompt medical attention does not become toti-potent. We have our people at all the medical information centers, and we get to a toti-potent case as soon as there is even a hint that such a case exists.

"But never mind that. My miracle is this: During my second phase I invented two little metal plates that, when fastened to the bottom of my shoes, enable me to walk on water. None of us know how those things work. We assume that I must have been in great danger from death by drowning, but we don't even know that. We can't duplicate them, although they appear to be constructed from the ordinary materials one might find aboard a ship. That is the real glory of it. This vast earth of ours, with its multitude of inventions apparently needs only a sharper mind to grasp at the facts that lie under our very eyes among the everyday things of life.

"Lesley, you know your task. Above ground you will find an assortment of machines. Engines, tools, electronic and electric instruments, something of almost everything.

Those dozen outbuildings are full of what seems to be junk, but isn't. Look them over. Let your mind try to create new combinations of those old forms. And the moment you have something, communicate with the men down here. They'll build anything you want in a few hours.

"Lesley, what we want, what the world must have, is a leader. Our own experience, our own purposes tell us that there is nothing to fear from such a development. Lesley, you will either be that leader, or you will be Jefferson Dayles' puppet, and the remaining thirty-four of us will be dead, because we would consider ourselves of no further value. Do you understand?"

As Craig was led to his bedroom, it seemed to him that their purpose couldn't have been expressed more clearly.

He kept awakening in a sweat of fear. Twice, lying in a half doze, he told himself he had dreamed his visit into the fortress under the ranchhouse. But each time a grimmer realization was there to chide his mind for its illusions. The day before, with the danger seemingly remote, he had dallied with the hope that they might actually be safe in this desert hideout. Now, he knew better. An army of tanks and planes would attack—and she and the others were determined to die if he failed to stop that attack, or if he was captured.

Craig jerked erect in bed. "Silly fool," he

thought furiously, "they won't do that; and yet I lapped it up."

The rage subsided as swiftly as it had come. He liked the woman. She had fire and an intense personality. And somehow—it had nothing to do with love—he couldn't imagine her dead.

Besides, it wasn't only she or the other totipotents whose lives were at stake. There were the blood slaves of them all, the people down below, who would build the machines he planned, all of them his blood type, depending on him for their immortality. How beautifully clever it all was, and how logical. They'd work like mad to carry out his plans.

And then there were the condemned killers. Odd to feel responsible for keeping *them* alive. Actually, of course, they shouldn't have been sentenced to death. People might hate the idea, but members of a mob were not first-degree murderers.

His mind twisted its uneven course through the long night. Once a wonder came: this twenty times average capacity of the human brain—it couldn't be I.Q. Only an electronic thinking machine could have an I.Q. of 2000. There were other factors in the brain that might be affected. How was it, for instance, that a person with an I.Q. of 100 frequently had twice the personality and leadership qualities of some freak with an I.Q. 150? No, the 20-brain wouldn't be I.Q. It would be—he couldn't imagine.

He must have slept on the thought. When he awoke, it was still dark, but there was decision in him. He would try. He felt no different, no greatness, but he would try.

As dawn broke, Jefferson Dayles rose and stared through the eye-holes of his flesh mask out through the window of Mountainside Inn. It was the waiting, he thought. All that he could do had been done. The orders, the intricate planning, the details of insuring that no escape avenues remained open—all that, he had attended to personally. And now others must do the work while he paced helplessly to and fro in the confines of this small room—waiting.

The door behind him opened, but he did not turn.

The shadows lay heavy on the desert, but the mountains to the right were visible against the lightening sky. And to the left among the scatter of trees beyond the village, he could see the white tents of the awakening army.

Kay said from behind him, "I've brought your breakfast."

He had forgotten that someone had come in. He jumped from the impact of the voice. And then smiled grimly at himself. He turned and said, "Breakfast?"

He drank his orange juice, and ate the kidney on toast in silence. When he had finished, Kay spoke again.

"I'm pretty certain no one suspects your presence." She added after a moment, "We'll start in about an hour. It will require at least three hours to cover the forty miles over the sand. Some of our scouts penetrated to within a few hundred yards of the house during the night without being challenged. However, they obeyed orders and made no attempt to invade the yard."

She finished, "I'm beginning to think our precautions have been ridiculous, but I agree that it's better to be sure than sorry. There is no longer any doubt. We must have this man before we can even think of a third term."

No answer. Four hours, Jefferson Dayles was thinking, four hours before he would know his fate.

CHAPTER 10

At the ranch, the chill of the desert night faded into a cold dawn which slowly warmed that gray land. The men were up early. They ate breakfast almost in silence, offered no objections to Craig's statement about the prisoner, and finally dispersed. Some went out to relieve the night watchers on the peaks that topped the gashed hills and uneven sand plains. Only one or two actually seemed busy.

The atmosphere was tense, nervous, expectant. As they closed the door of the third outhouse, Anrella said frowningly, "I certainly expected the men to object when you said that I would accompany you wherever you went today. It must have puzzled them."

Craig was silent. The mantle of leadership that had been yielded him puzzled him, too. Several times he had caught the beginning of opposition in the minds of the men, only to watch it fade away without being given expression. He grew aware that Anrella was speaking again, uneasily, "I wish I hadn't advised you to go back to sleep. We wanted you to be fresh for your task. But we also wanted to time everything so that you would have at least half a day."

Curiously, just like that, her words irritated him. He said sharply, "My means to success are too limited. And I have a conviction I'm approaching this whole subject from the wrong angle. It's the mechanical slant that's not right. I could see several possibilities, for instance, in the electrical equipment in that last outhouse. The use of the 999 plus vacuum offers several opportunities when conjuncted with electric coils but—"

He stared at her darkly. "There is one fatal flaw in them all. They kill. They burn and destroy. Frankly, I'll be hanged before I murder a bunch of poor soldiers doing their duty. And I might as well tell you right now I'm getting fed up. This whole business—" he waved his arm impotently—"is too silly for words. I'm beginning to wonder if I'm in my right mind." He scowled at her angrily. "Let me ask you a question. Is it possible for you to have a spaceship here in a short time to pick us all up and so save the lives of everyone above ground here?"

Anrella's gaze was quiet, her manner

tranquil. "It's even simpler than that. We could take you below ground. But the spaceship is available, too. There's one about twenty miles above us, a large model of what you used to think was an electric plane. I could call it down right now. But I won't. This is the critical moment in a plan we have been maturing ever since we first found you."

Craig snapped, "I don't believe your threat about killing yourselves. That's merely another pressure trick."

Anrella said softly, "You're tired, Lesley, and under great physical strain. I swear on my word of honor that what I have told you is the truth."

"What's ordinary honor to a superwoman?"

She was calm. "If you'll think about the implications of your refusal to kill the people who are coming to attack us, you will realize that what makes everything we do so right is that our intentions *are* honorable. And Lesley—I'm going to tell you something. I hadn't intended to. One of the two children with whom we experimented was—ours. Selection was by lot and—they cut off one of his legs and left him to become toti-potent. But instead, he died. The other one died, too. The reason we tried was because Martha Eger's grandson returned from the war toti-potent. It seemed to suggest, and actually it proved, higher potentiality but—we know now that isn't enough. Our blood will rejuvenate yet not 'start' the recipient's innate toti-potency.

"Lesley, I'll be eighty years old this year. Physically, of course, I don't feel it, but mentally I do. And so do the others. Seventeen of them are older than I am, twelve about the same age. It's strange that so few toti-potents came out of the last war; perhaps the medical services were better...but never mind that. All of us have seen a lot, thought a lot. And we feel sincerely that we can only be a hindrance to the human race unless we can somehow influence them along the paths of progress. To that end, we must have stronger, abler leadership than anything we have so far managed ourselves. We—"

There was a tiny *ting* from her magic jewel wrist radio. She lifted it, so that he could hear, too. A small but clear voice came:

"A column of armored cars and several tanks are streaming along the road that leads to Arroyo Pass ten miles south of Mountainside. A number of planes have been passing over here since dawn. If you haven't seen them, it must mean they're keeping out of sight of the ranch. That's all."

The minute *ting* repeated. And there was silence.

Anrella broke it in a strained voice, "I think," she said, "I think, Lesley, we had better get back to realities."

The shock grew. It wasn't the child, Craig told himself. That was too vague, although he caught himself in horrible visualization of the

118

fate of those two wretched children. The picture brought conviction, and, quite suddenly, he believed. Before he could speak, Anrella said anxiously:

"I'm beginning to think it's important that we have a preliminary weapon that will hold off land armies and give you time to develop a major invention. We won't have to worry about aerial bombing, because the last thing Jefferson Dayles desires is your destruction." She hesitated. "What about that disintegrating ray which affects only inorganic matter?" Her blue eyes gave him a quick, questioning glance. "We're willing to supply the wire to the nearest electric plug just as we did in the jail. Or even a mobile power plant." Once more she hesitated; then, "It would destroy their tanks, armored cars and would strip them to their birthday suits." She laughed nervously. "That would disorganize almost any army now in existence."

Craig shook his head. "I examined it just before breakfast. And it's no go. It's complete as is. I could reduce it to the size of a hand weapon and retain the same power. But an increase in bulk would add no energy. It all depends on one tube that—"

He shrugged. "All they have to do is verify that I'm not manning it, then keep their artillery beyond its quarter-mile range, and probe with high explosives. It's possible,"—he smiled savagely—"that one of the men would rather die that way than in a gas chamber.

But you can see it's no solution. What are you doing, Haines?"

They had come to where a well-set, unshaven young man was working on the engine of a car. The hood was up; and he was standing with one of the spark plugs in his fingers, brushing at its points. Actually, Craig's question was unnecessary. Clearly delineated in the man's mind was the intention to get the engine working, and leave the ranch.

Dan Haines was a bit-part actor, whose only reason for participating in the parade attack had been, as he had stated suddenly to the court, that he couldn't stand a "world run by women" and that he had "got excited". And also that he was ready to take "what was coming to him." He had added nothing to the escape except the burden of his jittery presence. And now, in a jump of apprehension, his nerve had broken. He looked up guiltily. "Oh!" he said as he saw Anrella. Then, more casually, "Just fixing the bus. I want us to be able to make a run for it if we have to."

Craig stepped past him, and stared down curiously at the exposed engine. In his mind's eye, he was visualizing the whole machine, first as a unit, then each separate function in detail. It was a lightning examination, and quickly paused there, and went back: battery—

He said slowly, "What would happen, Haines, if all the power of a battery was discharged in a hundred-billionth of a second?".

"Huh!" said Haines blankly. "That couldn't happen."

"It would," said Craig, "if the lead plate is electrically pre-hardened and if you use a pentagrid shielding tube, the type of tube that is used to control unwanted power. It—" He stopped, dazzled. The details stood sharp and clear in his mind. He made a mental calculation and then, looking up, saw Anrella's shining eyes on him.

After a moment, her gaze darkened. She said hesitantly, "I think I see what you're getting at. But wouldn't the temperature be too great? The figures I get are unbelievable."

"We can use a miniature battery," Craig said quickly, "not a full-sized one. After all, it's merely the percussion cap. The reason the temperature would be so high is that in the interior of a sun, there is no control tube, and so the right environment occurs only here and there through space, and we have a Nova-O sun.

"With a normal-sized battery the temperature would be too high. But I think we could strip off the four most dangerous oughts by using a small, short-lived dry cell, and so be safe." He turned away, frowning. Then paused, turned. *Don't* leave, Haines. Stay right here on the ranch."

"Yes, Mr. Craig."

Craig walked off thoughtfully; and then once more he stopped. "What," he thought, "was it the young man had said?"

Wide-eyed, he whirled and stared at Haines. The man had turned his back, but every mental contour of his brain was exposed. Craig stood there, comparing, remembering; and finally, satisfied, he faced Anrella and said quietly, "Let your people work on that at top speed. And work out, too, some refrigeration system for the ranchhouse. I think the battery should be buried about ten feet in the sand three or four miles south of here. And I don't see why it should take longer than three quarters of an hour. As for you and me—" He stared at her sardonically, "Order the spaceship down. We're going to Mountainside."

"We're what?" She looked at him, suddenly white. "Lesley, you know that doesn't follow logically out of this invention."

He made no answer, simply stared at her; and after a moment, she faltered, "This is all wrong. I s-shouldn't do it. I—" She shook her head, bewildered. Then without further protest, lifted her wrist radio.

By eight o'clock the old-timers were gathered on the porch at Mountainside Inn. Craig could see them looking slant-eyed at Anrella and himself and at the dozen very obvious secret service women who lounged in various positions around the door. The oldsters of Mountainside were not accustomed to having strangers intrude upon their privacy. But a danged lot of things had been happening lately. Their minds showed a mixture of excitement and irritation. Their conversation had a numbed quality.

It was about ten minutes after eight when one of them wiped the perspiration from his forehead and trotted to the thermometer beside the door. He came back. "Ninety-eight," he announced to his cronies. "Derned warm for Mountainside in February."

There was a brief, animated discussion on past heat records for the month. The cracked voices sagged slowly into an uncomfortable silence, as the hot breeze from the desert blew stronger. Once more an old-timer ambled to the thermometer. He came back, shaking his head. "Hundred and five," he said. "And it's only twenty-five minutes after eight. Looks like it's gonna be a scorcher."

Before Anrella could more than look startled, Craig walked over. "I'm a doctor," he said. "And sudden changes in temperature like this are pretty hard on older men. Go up to Mountain Lake. Make a day of it, a holiday. But go!"

When he came back to Anrella, they were already streaming off the veranda. They roared by a few minutes later in two old sedans. Anrella frowned at Craig. "The psychology of that was all wrong," she said. "Old desert rats don't usually accept the advice of younger men."

"They're not desert rats," said Craig. "They're lungers. And to them a doctor is God." He smiled and added, "Let's walk along the street a bit. I saw an old woman in a house there who ought to be advised to get into the hills."

The old woman was easily persuaded by a doctor to go on a picnic. She loaded some canned goods into a wheezy old car, and was off in a swirl of dust.

There was a meteorological station in a little white building fifty feet farther on. Craig opened the door and called to the perspiring man inside:

"What's the temperature now?"

The plump, bespectacled man dragged himself over to the desk. "It's 120," he moaned. "...Nightmare...The offices at Denver and Los Angeles are burning the wires asking me if I'm drunk. But"—he grimaced— "they'd better start redrawing their isobars, and warn their populations. By tonight the storm winds will be raising the seats of their pants."

Outside again, Anrella said wearily, "Lesley, please tell me what all this is about. If it gets any warmer, our flesh masks will float away on a river of perspiration."

Craig laughed grimly. It was going to get warmer, all right. He felt a sudden awe. A pinpoint of heat—he pictured it out there to the burning south—flashing eighteen million billion degrees Fahrenheit for one millionth of a second. The temperature here in Mountainside should go up to at least 135, and where the armored force was...145...150. It wouldn't kill. But the officers would surely order the army to turn back and race for the cool hills.

It was hotter as they headed back to the inn. And there were other cars moving towards the mountain highway, a long line of them. The heat shimmered above the sand and against the gray hillsides. There was a dry, baked scent in the air, a stifling odor, actually painful to the lungs. Anrella said unhappily, "Lesley, are you sure you know what you're doing?"

"It's very simple," Craig nodded brightly. "I consider we've got the equivalent of a good, roaring forest fire here. If you've ever seen a forest fire, and several of my memories include knowledge on the subject, you'll know that they flush every type of game from cover. There is a mad rush toward cooler territories. Even the king of the beasts condescends to run before such a conflagration. My guess was that we'd find a king here"—he finished smugly—"there he is now, out in the open, where I can make sure with a minimum of danger that I'm not fooling myself."

Craig nodded toward the inn door, from which a well-built man was emerging onto the veranda. The man's face was that of a very ordinary middle-aged American, but his voice when he spoke was the commanding, resonant voice of Jefferson Dayles.

"Haven't you got those motors going yet?" he asked irritably. "It seems strange, two cars getting out of order at the same moment."

There were mumbled exclamations of apology, and something about another car being along in a few minutes from the camp. Craig smiled, and whispered to Anrella:

"I see the pilot of your spaceship is still pouring down the interfering rays. O.K. Go ahead and issue the invitation."

"But he won't come. I'm sure he won't."

"If he doesn't come, it will mean I've been kidding myself, and we'll head straight back to the ranch."

"Kidding yourself about what? Lesley, this is life or death for us."

Craig looked at her. "What's this?" he mocked. "You don't like pressure? Maybe it will double your I.Q."

Without another word, she climbed the veranda steps.

He heard her disguised voice uttering the necessary words. As she finished, Craig called, "Yes, come. Your cars can follow."

The president and three secret agents followed Anrella down the steps. Anrella said steadily, "Do you think we can take four?"

"Oh, sure," said Craig. "One can squeeze in front here with us."

A minute later the car was in medium gear and purring up the first grade.

Craig said loudly, "You know, darling. I've been thinking about the Equalized women who make up the private army of President Dayles. The drug they took can be neutralized by a second dose, the chemical structure of which varies slightly from the original. The crystalline manganese element in the drug as it now is, is tied to the compound by four bars. That's unstable. By removing two of the bars, and I know just how it can be done, the connection will be stiffened. This will—"

He broke off as, from the corner of his eye, he saw the strained look on Anrella's face. From the rear seat, Jefferson Dayles said dryly, "Are you a chemist, Mr.— I didn't get the name."

"Craig," said Craig amiably. "Lesley Craig." He went on, "No, not a chemist. You can call me a sort of universal solvent. You see, I have discovered that I have a curious quality of the mind." He paused. In the rear-view mirror he saw the guns that the two agents in the back seat had drawn. Jefferson Dayles' voice came steadily:

"Go on, Mr. Craig."

"It is my determination," Craig said, "that President Dayles shall realize his ambitions; rejuvenation and continuation in the presidency until there has been re-integration of national and international morality on a much higher level than has ever prevailed. I favor, too, a progressively greater sharing of administrative power with women. This will require an educational program designed to—"

The stricken look on Anrella's face brought his first qualm of pity. But there was no such thing as explaining in the presence of others.

Haines' instant acceptance of his command had provided the clue. The rest—memory of how every command of determination he had expressed had been immediately acquiesced in—was confirmatory evidence. First, Peters bringing his clothes, and only afterwards questioning the act. Later, Anrella handing over the gun, and ordering the spaceship down, and the old men and old women going into the mountains—proved both men and women were subject.

It had nothing to do with the conscious mind. Not once had there been awareness. It went deeper. It affected some great basic nerve structure in the brain. It must seem to the obedient ones—their own logic.

An important angle, that last. Later, he would tell Anrella; now—there were commands to give that must sound like suggestions. He must make sure, for instance, that the army was recalled from its hell. Insure also that the agents put away their guns. And prepare for the storms that would be blowing down from the mountains to balance an unnatural cataclysm of weather.

Instant by instant, the future seemed brighter, more promising.

Craig gave the necessary orders as the car bowled down into a brief valley, and then up into the high, cool, sweet hills beyond.